UNWILLING ARMY

The winged creature was back. It dived down at Redbeard, screeching crazily and trailing its stream of fireballs. Donahoe hurled his warclub into the frothing face of the thing, and it vanished.

"Stop playing games with me!" he roared to Cole, shaking a fist in the direction of the tunnels. "Or I'll cut your heart out before nightfall!" Satisfied, he turned to the albino. "Tell Jeremy and Brin to fly to the edge of the mist. I want to know exactly where the Normans will break out."

"You can stay," the telepathic youth beside Donahoe said to the albino. "I just told them."

"Who asked you to?" snarled Donahoe. "Do what you're told, and keep your nose to yourself."

The youth opened his eyes, and Redbeard looked away bitterly. He resented the ungainly band of mutants that made up his army—resented them, but could do nothing about them. They were all fighting Gareth Cole's battle together. . . .

REDBEARD

Michael Resnick

PRESTIGE BOOKS • NEW YORK

REDBEARD

PRESTIGE BOOKS INC. • 18 EAST 41ST STREET
NEW YORK, N.Y. 10017

CHAPTER ONE

He was a misfit.

Gareth Cole knew it just by looking at him, of course. But the others were quick to learn.

When he was nine years old he went after his brother with a knife and hacked off both his heads. He very likely became the youngest rapist on record when he caught Julia Crane in one of the tunnels the next year, and his warclub had crusted blood on it before he reached his teens.

Gareth Cole not only permitted him to live—which he mistook for a mandate—but decided to put him to good use. At fifteen he led a raid against the Hub, and came out with half a dozen bloody heads hanging from his belt. It was almost a year later before he decided to scrape away the last vestiges of flesh from them.

He invaded the Hub and the Beach a dozen more times in as many years, and the fierce, bearded face of Red Will Donahoe was cursed a million times throughout the barren land.

It was a face that also did a lot of cursing of its own, most of which was aimed at Gareth Cole. He didn't mouth the curses aloud, but then, he didn't have to; Cole knew.

Donahue spat on the sand, wiped the flecks of saliva from the coarse red hair on his face, and glanced up. Circling overhead was an unearthly creature, birdlike in appearance, but sporting hideous leather wings and leaving a trail of fireballs in its wake. It cackled madly once, swooped down toward the river, then headed for the west.

"Get your blasted toys out of here!" growled Donahoe,

glaring after it.

"What was that?" asked the golden youth at his side.

"Nothing," muttered Donahoe. "I was just telling Gareth Cole what he could do with his damned monsters."

The youth closed his eyes and turned his face blindly in the direction of the tunnels.

"Gareth says to remind you that his birds will tell us when the Normans will launch their attack."

"When I need his help I'll ask for it!" snapped Donahoe, closing the subject. He turned his gaze back to the river. The mist would be lifting within an hour, and he didn't need the flaming creatures to know that the Normans would have to move across the water before then. There was the big tunnel too, but they'd tried it only once, years ago, and not one of them had returned home. Donahoe estimated the distance they would have to come once they passed through the mist. Three hundred, maybe three hundred and fifty yards. And those warships couldn't get the distance in less than five minutes—not with a thousand arrows streaking out at them.

He turned to the youth once more.

"To Rath with waiting for those birds. Go get Crag and tell him to look through the mist if he can."

The youth closed his eyes once more.

"Crag says there's too much light out. He can't see."

"Then tell him to get back to the tunnels. We have better things to do than protect a man with three blind eyes."

The youth nodded.

Donahoe surveyed his forces once more. The Normans would be silent, to be sure, but it wouldn't do any good. His men—he grimaced at the word—could fight a ten-year war without a single word spoken. Eccept by him.

A huge albino lumbered up to him, blinking his pink eyes and holding up a hand to shield them from the sun. He stopped before Donahoe and stared intently at

6

him.

"Well?" demanded the redbeard.

"I forgot," he stammered. Donahoe frowned at him. "They'll be here in a minute, sir."

"And how in Rath are you so blasted sure of that?" demanded Donahoe, although he knew the answer.

"I . . . I don't know. I just kind of feel it."

"All *I* feel is thirsty," said Donahoe.

"Gareth says to stop baiting him," said the youth, who had yet to reopen his eyes.

"You tell Gareth that when he can cut a man's bowels out like the rest of us, I'll take orders from him—and not until then!" roared Donahoe.

Then, suddenly, the winged creature was back. It dived down at the redbeard, screeching crazily and trailing its stream of fireballs with it. Donahoe slipped his war-club from his belt and hurled it full into the frothing face of the thing.

It vanished.

"You stop playing your idiot games with me," he roared, shaking a fist in the direction of the tunnels, "or I'll cut your heart out before nightfall!"

There was no answer and, satisfied, he turned back to the albino.

"Go to Jeremy and Brin and tell them to fly out to the edge of the mist. I want to know exactly where the Normans will break out."

"Yes, sir," said the albino and started off.

"You can stay," said the youth. "I've just told them."

"Who asked you to?" snarled Donahoe. "You do what you're told and keep your nose to yourself."

The youth opened his eyes at last.

"You may not like the power," he said evenly, "and Zameth knows you don't begin to understand it, but have the good sense to realize its value and utilize it while you may."

Donahoe glared at the youth, started to say something,

thought better of it, and stared back across the river again. The youth closed his eyes once more.

It would be only a minute or two now. The albino had said so, and he was never wrong. Zameth! The land was being invaded by Normans, and all he had to defend it with was this motley mixture of freaks and outcasts. He cursed under his breath and picked a large insect from his beard, split it with his nails, and discarded it.

The levitators entered the mist and soon emerged about ten feet above the water. Jeremy raised one of his hands—the indication that the attack was under way —and Brin pointed his only finger at the spot where the Normans would break through.

The flaming creature was back with its fiery tail, and Donahoe glared at it with a cold fury. "Get it out of here, Gareth! I'm not kidding!"

"Don't speak aloud," said the golden youth patiently. "He can hear you anyway, and all you're doing is letting the Normans know that we're waiting for them."

"If you'd open your damned eyes so you could see the Normans yourself, we just might have a better chance of defending ourselves," growled Donahoe.

"You know I'm more valuable in this capacity," replied the youth from behind his closed eyelids.

"Valuable!" exploded Donahoe. "There's not a one of you worth a tinker's damn, and that includes Gareth Cole! You're nothing but a bunch of freaks!"

The boy, who had been a youth for more than a century, merely sighed.

Suddenly they were interrupted by the twang of a thousand bowstrings, and Donahoe heard a score of Norman voices scream in pain and surprise.

"I told you to wait for my orders!" he bellowed, enraged.

"But Jon told us the order was given," said one of Jubal's heads.

8

"It's not given until you hear it from me!" thundered the redbeard.

"We killed sixteen of them," said the golden youth calmly, "and half a dozen more are drowning."

Donahoe broke off his tirade to scan the Norman forces. There were eight ships, all small enough to be manned by ten men and leave another fifteen free to return his fire.

The Normans had set up their crossbows and a few small catapults, and began bombarding the hills which housed Donahoe's men. One rock fell just to his left, crushing the albino's head.

"Return fire!" shouted the redbeard, walking over to take a warclub from the albino's corpse.

But before an arrow could be let loose, another Norman barrage landed amidst his men, scattering and maiming them.

"Ask Gareth to help us!" cried Jubal, all three of his heads for once in agreement.

Donahoe replied with an unintelligible curse.

"But there's no need to lose a single man!" pleaded Jubal.

Donahoe hurled a rock at Jubal's left head. Jubal ducked just in time, shuddering as it whizzed by his ear.

"I'm the commander!" bellowed the redbeard. "If there's anyone else who doesn't like it, say so now, before the Normans land!"

"I don't like it," said the golden youth.

"I've had about enough from you, Jon!" snapped Donahoe. He laid his hand to the hilt of his sword, but before he could withdraw it an arrow buried itself deep in the youth's shoulder.

"Keep down, you damned fool!" snarled Donahoe, throwing himself flat against the soil. "The next one might kill you!"

"The next what?" asked the youth, still not opening

his eyes.

"Zameth! Didn't you even feel it?"

"Feel what?"

The redbeard just stared at him with mouth agape.

The Normans were within fifty feet of the shore now, and Donahoe rose to his full height. "After me!" he bellowed, drawing his sword and racing down to the beach.

Behind him followed his forces. Not all of them ran, though; some flew, some loped, a handful of them slithered on their bellies, and Raal simply disappeared from his position and reappeared on the beach ahead of them all.

The Normans were abandoning their boats now, coming forth to meet the redbeard's hordes with swords, arrows, spears, and those odd, hook-shaped daggers they seemed to put so much stock in.

Donahoe chose the largest Norman he could find, a man who looked every inch his own brother, and closed with him. There was no finesse to his swordplay, no artistry to his footwork, just force and more force. He mouthed an endless stream of curses as he matched strength with his opponent.

Suddenly he saw an opening and, grabbing his huge broadsword in both hands, he swung it over his head and brought it down. Bits of hair and brain spattered his face, and he had to pause to withdraw his weapon from the carcass, using all his strength.

Then he was after another, whirling his blade about him like a dervish. He heard Brin crying for help, looked up, and saw the levitator plummeting toward the ground.

"Land on one of them!" shouted the redbeard. "You're done for anyway—take one of them with you!"

But Brin didn't hear, or perhaps he was beyond hearing. A moment later he lay still and lifeless on the sand, a trickle of blood running out of his ear.

The battle raged back and forth for only a few minutes. Then, slowly, the Normans retreated toward their ships. Donahoe sought out Jeremy, who was gazing blankly out to sea.

"Don't just stand there, you damned heathen!" he spat. "Fly out and put a torch to their ships! Let's cut off their retreat!"

Jeremy turned slowly to him and said nothing.

"Don't you understand? We can cut them off!"

Jeremy smiled pleasantly, then turned blindly back to the river.

Donahoe felled him with a single blow, then withdrew his club.

He needed fire, but how was he to get it? There simply wasn't enough time to find a flint, or enough dry wood.

The flaming creature swooped down toward him again, and one of the fireballs fell at his feet.

"By Zameth, no!" he screamed. "I'll do it without you!"

He stamped his sandaled foot down upon the fireball. The pain forced an oath from his lips, but he kept his foot there until the flame was extinguished.

Then, sheathing his sword and his warclub, he raced to the outskirts of the skirmish. No more than fifty yards separated him from the ships, and with a yell that would have startled even Gareth Cole, he raced into the pack of Normans.

He'd have been a lot safer with his sword drawn, but it would have slowed him down too much—and once he slowed down in the midst of the embattled Normans, he was as good as dead; his goal was to burst through them before they knew he was among them.

The first thirty yards were easy, as he bowled over the two Normans who stood in his way before they had a chance to bring their hooked daggers into play. Only one Norman remained in his direct path now, but this one was prepared.

Donahoe knew that if he took the time to dodge, the others would be upon him, so he lowered his head, bellowed one last curse at the top of his lungs, and charged full upon the man. The Norman sidestepped neatly and reached out with his hooked weapon, catching Donahoe just below the ribs.

The redbeard twisted forward, felt the metal cut through his side, heard the ripping of cloth and flesh— and then his way was clear. In another moment he was on the nearest of the ships.

Without bothering to see how many Normans were pursuing him, he raced to the anchor. It was held by a metal chain, and he turned his attention to the sails. He might cut them down, but the Normans would be upon him before he finished with the first of the ships —and besides, they had a dozen sets of oars on each ship in case the wind was unfavorable.

"All right! Give it to me!" he shouted into the wind. An instant later the flaming creature appeared again, depositing a fireball at his feet.

Donahoe thrust the wooden handle of his warclub into it, waited until the flame caught hold, and then applied it to the sails.

The wind caught the fire, urged it onward, and a moment later the mainmast was aflame as well. Donahoe went to the side of the deck, leaped to the next ship and repeated the process.

By the time the Normans had won enough breathing time to race to their boats, seven were aflame and Donahoe was applying the torch to the last of them. As the fire began eating across the rigging, an arrow whizzed past his head and he dived into the water, emerging some thirty yards beyond the northernmost ship.

His sword was too heavy to swim with, and he unbuckled the scabbard, letting it sink from sight. Then, filling his lungs with air, he disappeared beneath the surface once more.

When he broke through the surface this time, he was in shallow water, and he waded ashore, rejoining his forces a few hundred yards down the beach.

He stopped to rearm himself and walked over to Jon, who had not yet removed the arrow from his shoulder.

"What are our losses?" he demanded.

"Twenty-nine," replied the golden youth. "None of which was necessary."

"Open your eyes," growled the redbeard, "and see what's going on about you. The ships are on fire; not a single Norman will live to see this day end."

"Gareth could have done that without losing a man," said the youth, his eyes still closed.

"Zameth take you!" said Donahoe, and turned to his troups. "Retreat to the high ground and use your arrows!"

The retreat was as ungainly and grotesque as the charge, but soon those that survived it were safely behind their barricades, bombarding the hapless Normans with thousands of arrows.

When the last of them lay dead upon the sand, Donahoe turned to the youth.

"Tell Gareth we'll be home in two hours," he said.

"He knows."

"Tell him anyway!"

The redbeard walked off in a rage. He went down to the blood-soaked sand, drew his sword, and decapitated the largest and ugliest of the corpses. Then, inserting a finger beneath his belt, he drew the hair of the head through and knotted it securely.

The flaming creature hovered above him, observing him intently. Donahoe searched about for a rock, found one, and flung it at the firebird. The creature fluttered its leather wings to ward off the stone, but it caught the firebird on the side of the skull, dazing it.

And, in the tunnels, a man placed a hand to his temple and moaned.

13

CHAPTER TWO

Gareth Cole arose from his chair and stretched. It was a rather impotent action. He stood barely five feet tall, and stretching only emphasized the fact. He brushed a thick shock of blond hair back off his forehead and stared at the door.

Red Will Donahoe was coming. He had followed the redbeard's progress for the better part of an hour, and he knew exactly what was on his mind—though Cole hesitated to call such a morass of raw, untutored emotions a *mind*.

Donahoe approached the door, and Cole instructed his sentry to let him in.

"I ought to nail your skin to the wall!" roared the redbeard.

"I sincerely doubt that you could," said Cole calmly, "although you're certainly welcome to try."

Donahoe fingered his warclub. "I'm warning you, Gareth! Keep away from me. If you don't like the way I handle your army, get someone else—but don't meddle!"

"To answer your question, I couldn't possibly care less how you handle your warriors, barbarian."

"Then leave me alone!"

"If I were to leave you alone, your own people would kill you within a week."

"My own people!" exploded the redbeard. "My own people! They're nothing but freaks!"

"Poor barbarian," said Cole, and he almost allowed a trace of emotion to creep into his voice. "In most ways, any one of them is worth a dozen of you. Can you levitate like Jeremy? Or see infrared vibrations like Crag? Or—"

14

"Or fall asleep on my feet like Jeremy does in the heat of battle, or turn blind in the daylight like Crag?" said Donahoe contemptuously. "Can any of them hurl a club or swing a sword without my goading and prodding them? Can they take a woman? Zameth! We've even got a few who'd shrivel up and die if I plucked them from the water! And you've only named the handful that actually can *do* something. The rest of them look like they were slapped together by chance. What can Jubal do with three heads except argue himself to sleep each night? Or how about Keith? What can he do with one leg and four arms? And you—a strong wind would blow you over!"

"I think not," said Gareth Cole calmly. "*I make the winds.*"

"Yes," said the redbeard. "You make the winds and you create firebirds and you call your nameless monsters up from Rath. Well, you may scare the others, but you're not scaring Red Will Donahoe!"

"I don't scare anyone," corrected Cole. "Which is not to imply that I can't."

"If you've got so much blasted power," sneered Donahoe, "why don't you destroy the Normans?"

"It's all so trivial," sighed Cole. "I wish I could care what happens to you and the Normans, but it's just too insignificant. I have so little time, and you expect me to care about how beautiful you find the Norman women or whether Crag can see in the daylight."

"If you don't care about it, then don't interfere."

"You realize, of course, that you didn't have to lose a single man," said Cole. "It was sloppily done."

"I lost less than thirty men and killed four hundred Normans," said the redbeard defensively.

"You didn't answer me," noted Cole.

"I didn't lose any *men!*" snapped Donahoe. "I lost a thing that flies through the air, and a giant with no color on his skin, and a freak that crawled on its belly

15

—but no *men!*"

"The freak that slithered on its belly—as you so delicately put it—was a man who could transmit and receive thoughts at a distance of five thousand miles," replied Cole. "You, barbarian, can't do the same at five inches. Brin was able to levitate through the mist and tell you exactly where the Norman attack would come from. Could you do as much?"

"Who beat the damned Normans?" raged Donahoe. "Who hacked them apart and set fire to their ships?"

"Who gave you the fire?" countered Cole. "You couldn't even do that without my help. Besides, if you had the slightest inclination toward practicality, you'd have had Raal teleport himself to the deck and set the fire. It would have saved you that," he added, pointing to the deep gash on Donahoe's side.

"If you can do any better," said Donahoe, "why don't you lead them in battle yourself?"

"I do."

"What are you talking about?" demanded the red-beard. "I give the orders!"

"But have you ever stopped to think why they should obey you? Have you ever wondered what they say behind your back?"

"They don't say anything."

"Nothing that you could hear," agreed Cole. "But you will admit that you're hardly the kind of man they'd be willing to die for."

"And I suppose you are?"

"As a matter of fact, yes."

"You just keep your nose out of the next one and I'll prove to you that they'll obey anyone. They haven't the gumption not to."

"I'm afraid you would be in for a disappointment. They obey you only because I tell them to."

"You're a liar!"

"Am I? Why do you think they do your bidding—

16

because you carry human heads around with you? In fact, when you get down to facts, why do they even let you survive? Take last week when you raped Maria Wills." Donahoe uttered a low curse. "Do you really think I didn't know about it? Or that she couldn't communicate with us even though you held your hand over her mouth? It went unpunished only because I decided it would go unpunished."

"Zameth, what a world!" bellowed Donahoe furiously. "What a world of freaks and idiots!"

"It is a world in which you are an inferior," said Cole. "Be thankful that it has allowed you to live. And, more to the point, thank me that *I* have allowed you to live, for even your parents wanted you destroyed at birth."

"I don't even know who my parents are," said Donahoe. "Nobody in the tunnels does."

"That's not quite true. Nobody in the tunnels is told, but a few of us know. I do. So does Jon. The reason none of you is told is that we have not begun breeding true yet."

"What in Rath is that supposed to mean?"

"I should think you of all people would know."

"Why me?"

"Because you are an outsider, a throwback, a mutant in reverse."

"I don't know what you're talking about. Who were my parents?"

"Do you really want to know?"

Donahoe considered it carefully. What if his father was Jubal, or Jeremy, or even Jon?

Or worse yet—what if his father was Gareth Cole?

"No," he muttered at last.

"I thought not. Anyway, it was unanimously decided that you be put to death in infancy, but I overruled them."

"You'll regret it yet," promised the redbeard.

"I never experience regret," replied Cole. "No, I could

17

see even then the factors which would someday make you invaluable to me."

"And now I've proved it!" said Donahoe, giving the head attached to his belt a fond pat.

"You've done nothing of the kind," corrected Cole. "As I said, you could have won without a single casualty. Between your battles and your life in the tunnels, you have contributed to more than two hundred of our deaths. Surely you've done nothing to be proud of yet."

Donahoe just stared at him.

"Don't look so surprised, barbarian. I don't begrudge you your bloodlust. It was there at the moment of your birth, and it has never diminished. I knew that, and I foresaw what would come of it. Nonetheless, there will come a day when I will need you above all else; it is because of this that you have survived in a society that has no place for you."

"I'll die before I go a step out of my way to help you!" hissed the redbeard.

"We shall see," said Cole with an enigmatic smile.

"Bring on your monsters right now!" challenged Donahoe, working himself up into a killing fury.

"They'll be here when I need them—and they're not all monsters, you know."

"Don't give me that. I've seen them!"

"Did you ever think that you might seem a monster to, say, Jubal? After all, you've only got one head, and you can't fly, and you're not a telepath, and . . ."

He got no farther, for the redbeard picked up a chair and hurled it at him. Before it could strike its target, a huge, resilient web sprung miraculously from the air, caught the chair and flung it back into Donahoe's face.

The redbeard collapsed with a grunt, but was on his feet an instant later, warclub in hand.

"I wouldn't advise it," said Cole calmly. "You may not understand it or admit it, but we two need each other."

"Why should you need *me?*" demanded Donahoe sullenly. "Why not Jon or Jeremy or one of the others?"

"I have no intention of putting you on your guard by telling you," said Cole. "But it should be obvious that there isn't a thing the others can do that I can't. I have all their talents combined in a single mind, as well as some they can never have."

"Then, in Zameth's name, why don't you destroy the Normans?"

"As I told you before, I have more important things to do—and besides, I have nothing against the Normans."

"Nothing against them?" exploded the redbeard.

"No. After all, they were here first."

"What are you talking about?"

"I drove them out of the tunnels centuries ago," said Gareth Cole.

CHAPTER THREE

He had been in an ugly mood when he left the tunnels, and now, as he peered through the heavy mists three days later, it had become appreciably uglier.

"Damn his bones to Rath!" he muttered for the thousandth time. And for the thousandth time he cast an apprehensive glance skyward to see if Gareth was sending one of his firebirds in retaliation.

But no, Gareth wouldn't do that. It wasn't like him to display any emotion, any anger. Dimly, and only after many years, the redbeard had begun to appreciate Gareth Cole's subtlety. Firebirds? Never. He'd be far more likely to send a gust of wind against Donahoe's accouterments; not enough to hurt him, but more than enough to give his position away.

The redbeard picked up a dry leaf, ground it to powder in his massive fist, then released it to test the wind. He knew the Normans kept dogs in their camps, and he wasn't about to get downwind of them.

He peered ahead again, silently cursing the limited visibility. Zameth! He *had* to be within fifty yards of them by now, and still he could see nothing. He placed his hand to the hilt of his sword and moved stealthily forward.

You just watch, Gareth. Watch and see what a man *can do!*

He crept forward, one step at a time, wondering how many Normans might be just ahead of him. It didn't really matter, though. No Norman had ever been able to survive his sword, and none ever would. An involuntary shudder raced through his body as the cold moisture from the air settled upon him.

He had been walking for three days, looking for Normans upon whom to vent his spleen. He would continue walking straight to the Hub, and Zameth help any man who stood in his way. He didn't need Gareth Cole or anyone else to help him kill Normans, and he was damned well going to prove it once again.

A low growl off to his left brought him to sudden attention. He started to draw his sword, decided that the grating noise as it slid out of the sheath would be too loud, and instead pulled his warclub out of his belt. Another snarl came to his ears, but the mist was too thick to see where it emanated from.

Then, suddenly, a huge mass of hair and teeth and bone hurled itself upon his back, forcing an inadvertent oath from his lips. He shook his massive shoulders and felt the dog fly off, only to have it leap for his throat an instant later. He reached out with his left hand, locked his fingers around the animal's throat, and brought his club down upon the head time and again, shattering it first and then turning it into a sticky jelly. With a final curse, he flung the carcass away from him and looked quickly around for the Normans.

Surely they couldn't have helped hearing the brief but frenzied battle, and yet he couldn't perceive a single form in the darkness. Where were they? Were they still awaiting the outcome, unsure as to whether man or beast had emerged victorious? Or had he been completely erroneous about their location—had the mists confused his sense of direction?

He tightened his grip on his warclub and began advancing again. Then he saw it: a single tent beside the dying embers of a small fire.

With a scream designed to frighten his opponents into immobility, he charged down upon the canvas dwelling, slashing the side open with his sword and leaping into the center of it.

It was empty. And yet the remnants of the fire proved

21

they had been here recently, as did the dog. They must be hiding then, waiting for him to go elsewhere in search of Norman blood. Well, he wouldn't be fooled or discouraged this easily; he had left the tunnels to prove once again to Gareth Cole that he could singlehandedly walk into the center of the Hub, could slay more Normans than Gareth's entire army and take more women than they'd ever dreamed of, and by Zameth he was going to!

He stepped out into the open, standing by the remains of the fire where he hoped he could be seen.

"Come on out!" he thundered into the mist. Then, with slow, exaggerated motions, he unhooked his belt and scabbard, letting them fall noisily to the ground. "See? I need no weapons against the likes of you! Now, show yourselves!"

He stood motionless, waiting. The mist was thick, but he could see a good twenty feet ahead of him. His battle-hardened muscles were tense and ready, and he clenched his hands until the fingers left deep indentations in his palms. He licked his lips as he imagined the feel of a Norman throat beneath those fingers. He smiled grimly; he was content.

Then he heard them. The sound was very slight, just a tiny twig breaking directly behind him; but twigs don't break of their own accord, and so he slowly bent his legs, ready to leap aside instantly. The sound had come from perhaps forty feet away, and he knew he'd be able to hear a rush from twenty. Therefore, the man still had to be approaching cautiously. Well, let him be as cautious as he wanted, just as long as he came within reach—

An arrow thudded home into the redbeard's shoulder. He collapsed on his face, the shock and force of the wound and the fall knocking his breath from him.

"Good shot, Elston!" cried an elated voice.

"Sitting, duck," came the calm reply.

22

Donahoe tried to rise to face his antagonists, found that he couldn't, and turned his head, trying to make out the advancing figures through the darkness of the night and the red haze of pain that was rapidly engulfing him.

"Is it Cole?"

"No such luck," replied the one named Elston. "But I think we've got his henchman."

"I'm no henchman!" hissed the redbeard, trying unsuccessfully to focus his eyes. A booted foot swung out of the night, catching him on the jaw and spinning him over onto his side.

"Shut up, Donahoe!" snapped the man named Elston. "We know full well who you are, worse luck for you. What are you doing here anyway, so far from the protection of the elusive Mr. Cole?"

"I'm not so far," grated the redbeard. "He can kill you whenever he wants."

"Oh, really?" said Elston in a bemused tone of voice. "Then why don't you call for help?"

"Wouldn't . . . give him . . . the pleasure," spat Donahoe, and fainted.

"Well, Michael," said Elston, "what do you say—shall we finish him off here or bring him back with us?"

"Considering what he's capable of doing, I'd ordinarily say don't take any chances," replied the man named Michael; "but he's not going to be lopping any heads off for a few days with that arrow in him, and besides, we might be able to get some information out of him."

"If Gareth Cole doesn't get to him first," replied Elston grimly.

"Do you really think he can reach this far?" asked Michael skeptically.

"Hard to say. I don't really think people can create tangible monsters out of empty air either, and yet I've seen him do it."

"What about our friend here?" asked Michael, indicat-

23

ing the redbeard. "If we're going to take him prisoner instead of killing him, we'd better stop the bleeding."

"I suppose so," agreed Elston, kneeling down beside the still figure. He let out a low whistle. "Take a look at the scars this fellow carries around with him! Hell, if he could survive some of those, this arrow probably feels like a pinprick to him!"

"The arrow may not bother him too much," said Michael clinically, "but I'd guess that he's lost damned near a quart of blood."

"Well, enough talking," said Elston. "Time to get down to business." With that, he reached down, grabbed the shaft of the arrow, braced a foot against the redbeard's ribcage, and pulled.

"Ugly wound," commented Michael as the arrow finally came away.

"Ugly character," replied Elston coldly. "Can't say he didn't have it coming to him."

"Looks just like one of us," said Michael, scrutinizing Donahoe's features. "One head, two arms, two legs . . ."

"I guess every now and then they get one."

"I was just wondering," said Michael. "If there's one, do you suppose . . . ?"

"I doubt it. We'd have known of it long before now."

"I guess you're right," shrugged Michael. "Lend a hand and we'll carry him over to the tent. We can tie him up there and make a stretcher out of the canvas."

Donahoe came to his senses as they raised his body upright and began dragging him to the tent. His left arm was hanging limply by his side, and before they knew he was awake he had rammed his fist into Michael's groin. The man doubled over in pain and began vomiting, but before Donahoe could wrench free, he felt the sharp slap of an open hand against his still-bleeding wound and once again he tumbled headlong onto the ground.

"Are you all right, Michael?" asked Elston. Michael,

still vomiting, nodded his head weakly. "Well," he said, picking up a dead tree limb and pressing it to Donahoe's shoulder, "we won't make *that* mistake again."

"Who are you?" grated the redbeard, trying to squirm away from the stick.

"I am Baron Elston Stramm, and the young man you almost unsexed is Michael Drake. Do our names mean anything to you?"

"Should they?" muttered Donahoe.

"In all modesty, I must answer in the affirmative. You see, the two of us have killed almost as many of your people as you have of ours."

The redbeard growled an incoherent oath. "They're not my people!"

"Oh?" chuckled Stramm. "And I suppose you've never heard of Gareth Cole either."

"Someday I'll kill him," said the redbeard softly. "After I kill you."

"Your mind seems to run in a rut," said Stramm easily. "I doubt that you'll live long enough to kill anyone."

"We'll see," said Donahoe, his eyes glowing like blazing coals.

"You're a friendly one, aren't you? I wonder that your people have put up with you for so long."

"I told you before: they're not my people."

"Of course they are. You're no better—and no different—from the rest of them."

"I'm all right now," said Drake, returning. He turned to Donahoe. "I'll get you for that, mutant, if it's the last thing I ever do!"

"What did you call me?" snapped the redbeard.

"I called you mutant," said Michael Drake, just before he brought a stick down on Donahoe's shoulder and obliterated all consciousness.

CHAPTER FOUR

"He's waking up now."

"So this is the notorious Red Will Donahoe. Phew! He smells like he hasn't washed in a year."

"Probably hasn't. I'm still amazed that he survived that wound."

"He'll wish he hadn't."

Donahoe slowly opened his eyes. He was lying flat on his back, his arms and legs strapped to a cot. The air was damp and musty. He looked around, blinking, and saw that he was in a large stone room. A little trickle of water ran down the wall directly behind his head, culminating in a stagnant, foul-smelling puddle on the dirt floor. He thought he could hear the scraping of a small rodent somewhere off to his right, but if so, it was out of his line of vision.

Standing above him, looking down with almost scientific detachment, were Stramm and another Norman he didn't recognize. Now, for the first time, he had a chance to scrutinize Stramm's features. The man was tall, almost as tall as the redbeard, though his body was built along far more slender lines. His black hair was cut short, and was beginning to recede at the temples, leaving him with a very noticeable widow's peak. Two dark eyes, a prominent hooked nose, and a neatly-manicured goatee completed the picture.

The other man, clothed in the cloth and leather trappings typical of the Normans, was blond and relatively nondescript, save for a deep scar running from his forehead down to the corner of his mouth.

"Good morning, mutant," said Stramm sardonically. "I trust you slept well."

Donahoe glared at him, but said nothing.

"I'll take your silence as an affirmative," continued Stramm. "And now, you are going to answer some questions."

"That's what you think," growled Donahoe.

"That's what I *know*," replied Stramm, leaning down on the redbeard's injured shoulder and causing the blood to flow again. Donahoe groaned and Stramm withdrew the pressure. "I can keep this up as long as you can, with considerably less wear and tear. Now, are you prepared to be reasonable?"

Donahoe sullenly nodded his head.

"Fine. The gentleman standing next to me is Baron Gerald Rysler. Since we found you on his property, we thought it only diplomatic that he be asked to join our little session. Suppose you begin by telling us what you were doing there?"

"Looking for Normans," responded the redbeard defiantly.

"Were you indeed? And what, pray tell, might a Norman be?"

Donahoe turned his head and spat on the floor.

"Come, come," said Stramm, prodding his shoulder with the flat side of a hooked sword. "That's hardly an answer."

"It's the only one you're getting!" bellowed Donahoe, spitting once more and hitting Stramm's boot with it.

"An interesting crop of warriors Gareth is producing this season," commented Rysler dryly.

"Gareth Cole didn't produce me!" snapped the redbeard. "I never needed him before, and I don't need him now!"

"You said much the same thing when we captured you last night," commented Stramm. "Why?"

"None of your blasted business!"

"Ah, but it is," replied Stramm, slapping the sword down on Donahoe's shoulder again. "After all, if you're

27

not on friendly terms with Gareth Cole, why do you lead his armies for him—and, more to the point, what were you doing when we captured you?"

"I told you: I was looking for Normans."

"And now, if you don't want me to slice your arm completely off, I think you had better tell me just what a Norman is."

"*You're* a Norman."

"Just me?" inquired Stramm.

"No. All of you."

"All of who?"

"Everyone who doesn't live in the tunnels."

"And those who *do* live in the tunnels—what do you call them?"

"I call them scum!" snapped Donahoe, staring at the stagnant puddle and the roaches that scurried around it.

"If you should ever survive and return to your scummy friends," said Stramm, "you might tell your beloved Mr. Cole that the word is *Normal*, not Norman."

"What are you talking about?" demanded the redbeard.

"*I'm* asking the questions, mutant. Now, why were you hunting for us?"

"To kill you," replied Donahoe, surprised by the question. "Why else would I hunt Normans?"

"Why were you alone?" demanded Rysler. "We know you're Cole's general. Where was his army?"

"Roasting in Rath, for all I give a damn!"

"Rath?" repeated Rysler. "What does that—"

"Gerald, I think we could spend years trying to interpret his jargon," interrupted Stramm. "Let's get back to the main point."

"But if this Rath is somewhere nearby . . ." protested Rysler.

"Let me get my hands on you and you'll find out where it is, all right!" said Donahoe ominously.

28

"I see," said Rysler, his eyes lighting up. "It's his word for hell."

"So it seems," agreed Stramm, slapping at a large insect. "All right, mutant," he said turning back to the redbeard. "Why did you come here alone?"

"To kill Normans."

"Then why not lead your army?" insisted Stramm. He prodded Donahoe with the sword. "I am fast losing my patience with you. I expect a straightforward answer."

"To show Gareth Cole that I don't need him or his freaks to kill Normans!" Donahoe twisted his head as the edge of the blade came to rest across his throat.

"You seem to possess as passionate a distaste for Cole as we do. Why?"

"None of your business!"

The blade lowered a fraction, and Donahoe felt his skin splitting.

"I don't care what you do to me!" he spat. "You leave Gareth Cole out of this! I did this without him, do you understand?"

"Is he protecting Cole?" asked Rysler calmly, as he watched a thin trickle of blood spread across the redbeard's throat.

"I don't think so," said Stramm, removing the sword. "As I mentioned, he seems to bear no great love for him."

"Then why does he fight for him?" asked Rysler.

"I don't know. Ask him," replied Stramm.

"You heard the question, mutant," said Rysler. "If you hate Cole as you say you do, why do you remain with him?"

"Because I hate Normans too!" bellowed Donahoe.

Stramm sat down on the cot beside Donahoe, grasped the massive beard, and pulled it until he was staring directly into Donahoe's face. "Listen to me," he said slowly, carefully enunciating each word. "The penalty for invading our land is death; in your case, death by

29

slow and extremely painful torture. If you've any desire whatsoever to avoid it, you'd better tell us everything you know about Cole right now."

"Cole!" spat the redbeard. "Cole! Damn it, man, *I'm* the one who's been defeating your armies, not Cole!"

"I've no more time for your delusions of grandeur," said Stramm. "You tell me what Cole's weaknesses are or you're a dead man."

"How do I know you won't kill me anyway?" demanded Donahoe, flinching as a drop of water fell from the ceiling and landed on his eyelid.

"You don't—but you know what will happen if you refuse to answer. Besides, if you hate Cole half as much as you claim to, you ought to be happy to help us."

"I'll kill him myself," growled the redbeard. "I don't need your help."

"You need all the help you can get right now," said Stramm. "Now, what are Cole's weaknesses?"

"He hasn't got any," replied Donahoe sullenly.

"Every man has weaknesses," said Stramm. "Have you ever tried to find them?"

"Every day of my life."

"What are his vices?" said Rysler.

"None."

"No weaknesses and no vices?" said Stramm mockingly. "You make him sound almost godlike."

"I haven't noticed any Normans discovering what makes him tick," shot back the redbeard.

"True," admitted Rysler. "In fact, no one in our generation has so much as seen him—or if they have, they haven't returned to tell about it."

"Yet the man must have a flaw somewhere," persisted Stramm. "If not, why hasn't he wiped us out already? Answer that one, mutant."

"My name is Donahoe, not mutant."

"Your name is anything I say it is," replied Stramm,

stroking another thin red line along his throat. "Answer the question, mutant."

"I don't know. He says he's too busy."

"Too busy doing what?"

"I don't know."

"It couldn't be that he can't send his creatures this far, could it?" said Rysler. "That his powers diminish over a distance?"

"He can reach you, all right," replied Donahoe with certainty.

"If he can reach *us*, it stands to reason he can reach *you*," said Stramm. "Why doesn't he?"

"None of your—" The blade cut in again, more painfully this time. "Because he's waiting for me to ask him. Because he enjoys seeing you stick that sword into me."

"Then why does he let you live?" demanded Stramm.

"Because he needs me."

"Why?"

"No one else could bring any order to that bunch of freaks he calls an army."

"That's not good enough, mutant," said Stramm. "Gareth Cole doesn't need you or anyone else to fight his wars for him." Donahoe flushed but remained silent, and Stramm continued. "Out with it now: what's your special power?"

"Let me up off this cot and you'll see!" promised Donahoe.

"I'm not talking about your strength. What else do you have that he needs?"

"I don't know what you're talking about," said the redbeard.

"We know he's got levitators and telepaths and God knows what else. What's *your* specialty? What qualifies *you* to lead his army?"

"Because I'm the only man he's got with the guts to do it!"

31

"Those guts will soon be strewn all over the floor if you don't come up with a better answer."

Donahoe glared balefully up at Stramm. He strained once again at his bonds, found them as taut as ever, and collapsed back on the cot, grimacing at the pain in his shoulder. The water began dripping on him again.

"*All right,*" he said softly.

"What?" demanded Stramm. "I didn't hear you."

"*He* did," muttered the redbeard with an air of defeat.

"He? You mean Rysler?"

"No, I don't mean Rysler. I mean Gareth Cole, damn him!"

"You think he heard you?" persisted Stramm.

"I know it."

"He's almost two hundred miles away."

"He could be on the moon for all I give a damn!" snapped Donahoe.

"And yet you think he's going to help you?"

"Wait and see," said Donahoe forebodingly.

Suddenly they heard a laugh coming from behind them. Stramm turned and saw a firebird hovering six feet above the ground. It opened its beak and Gareth Cole's voice came out.

"It will be a long wait, barbarian," it said, and vanished.

CHAPTER FIVE

The Council of Barons was meeting in the spacious dining hall of Gerald Rysler's castle. The fog had lifted, and the cold glow of the moon permeated the candlelit room. Five men were seated around a table while their knights and squires lined the walls, standing rigidly at attention. Five men, who juggled the destiny of their race in their hands . . .

"I'm flatly against it," Stramm was saying. "I don't think we should even consider it."

"I agree with Elston," said Michael Drake. "It took us fifteen years to capture him, and now you want to turn him loose again."

"Not loose," said Baron Aldan Povich. "Not loose, Michael. I don't think that was what Gerald meant to imply at all." The oldest of the assembled Barons, he was nonetheless the most physically impressive, towering above even Donahoe. It always surprised Drake to hear him speak with his gentle lisp, or to realize that he spent most of his time away from the battlefield tending to his gardens.

"Of course I didn't mean to imply that," snapped Rysler from the head of the table, "and you know it, Michael! I'm simply trying to carry this thing through to its logical conclusion."

"And is it logical to turn the mutant loose so that he can go on killing us?" demanded Drake hotly.

"That's not what I'm suggesting," replied Rysler, trying to keep his temper in check. "All I know is that he seems to bear some kind of grudge against Gareth Cole, and I don't see why we can't turn it to our own advantage."

"How do you know that?" asked the youngest of the Barons, Andrew Craston. Craston had been blinded by one of Gareth Cole's firebirds while still a child. He was not a forgiving man. "How do you know it's not just an act, a cover-up to force us into the very blunder you're contemplating?"

"I *don't* know, damn it!" exploded Rysler. "But I think we should look at all sides of the problem."

"There's only one side," said Craston coldly. "Kill him." Then, as an afterthought, he added, "Slowly."

"Just a minute," interrupted Povich. He leaned forward and his great bulk threw an awesome shadow across the wooden table. "Whatever else we do, we must act with unanimity. Gerald has made a suggestion; I move that we hear him out."

"Thank you," said Rysler. "Now, as I see it, there are three main questions: first, why did Donahoe come here alone; second, does he really hate Cole, and if so, why; and third, why doesn't Cole rescue him? If these items, especially the last two, are answered to my satisfaction, I'll withdraw my proposal."

"The first one's easy enough," said Drake. "He came here for the very reason he gave: to kill Normals."

"That's not good enough, Michael," said Stramm. "The question was not as to his purpose; I think we all agree on that. But why did he come alone? And if his answer—that he's feuding with Cole and wanted to prove his ability—holds up, then why did he pick our strongest position? Why not some poorly manned outpost?"

"Because he's a hotheaded egomaniac," replied Drake. "You remember when he found us, Elston: the first thing he did was disarm himself and offer to fight us bare-handed. That kind of mentality would naturally lead him to walk right into the center of the Hub without ever considering the possibility of defeat."

"That seems to make sense, Michael," lisped Povich, lighting a large pipe and inhaling the strong-smelling

34

smoke. "Would your observations agree with that conclusion, Elston?"

"Perhaps," said Stramm noncommitally.

"Then go on to your second question, Gerald," said the old man, puffing away industriously.

"I'll repeat it," said Rysler. "Does Donahoe really hate Gareth Cole?"

"How can you answer that?" snapped Drake disgustedly. "How can you be sure?"

"If he hated him, would he still be Cole's general?" inquired Craston sardonically.

"I think you're attacking this the wrong way," interjected Stramm. "Michael's right when he says we have no way to check out Donahoe's statement. I think that we should, for the sake of argument, assume he's telling the truth and try to figure out *why* he and Cole are enemies."

"There isn't any reason!" said Drake impatiently. "Hell, when you get past Cole, he's the most powerful man they've got."

"Isn't that reason enough?" asked Povich pointedly. "Is the second-in-command ever truly satisfied with his station?"

"He'd have to be," replied Drake. "Nobody is going to dethrone Cole."

"How do you know?" said Stramm suddenly. "How do you know that isn't precisely what's going on?"

"What are you talking about, Elston?" said Drake, surprised. "You've seen him. Does he look like another Gareth Cole to you? The man doesn't have anything but muscle. He looks just like one of us."

"So does Gareth Cole," pointed out Rysler. "That's why they let him live in the first place."

"I agree with Gerald," said Stramm. "And the mere fact that he hasn't used any mutated powers to escape doesn't mean he doesn't possess them."

"But you were just seconds from killing him," insisted

35

Drake. "And yet he didn't make a move to disarm you or protect himself."

"Maybe he could read my mind and tell it was a bluff," said Stramm. "Or perhaps he only needs a fraction of a second to disarm me; maybe he was waiting for the last possible instant before showing us any powers he wanted to keep secret."

"I can accept that within the framework of this discussion," said Povich, blowing great rings of smoke as he spoke. "But even if that's true, Elston, that hardly accounts for his appearance in Gerald's fields. What was he doing there?"

"I agree with Michael on that point," said Stramm. "I honestly believe he was hunting for us."

"Then we come to a contradiction," continued Povich. "How is it that a man who may be the equal of Gareth Cole allowed himself to be caught and almost killed before he had slain a single one of us?"

"*Maybe he wanted to be caught,*" said Craston, staring blindly across the table.

"What?" exclaimed Drake incredulously.

"Maybe he wanted to be caught," repeated Craston. "How can you be sure this isn't all part of some plan of Gareth Cole's—or even Donahoe's, if he has the powers you seem to be attributing to him? How do you know that they couldn't forsee that we'd act in precisely this way?"

There was a momentary silence, broken only by the hooting of a screech-owl just outside the window, as the other four Barons considered Craston's statement.

"You may have something there, Andrew," said Povich at last. "I had never considered the possibility before, but it's quite possible that Gareth Cole sent him here and allowed him to be caught, though I'm not sure why he'd do such a thing."

"I am," said Drake decisively. "He knew one of us would suggest, as Rysler did, that Donahoe might be of more use to us alive than dead. Then he probably instructed Donahoe to act as if he was at war with him in the hope that we'd form just the kind of idiot plan that we seem to be considering."

"Michael's right," said Craston. "We're being manipulated like pieces on a gameboard. Cole is applying pressure and we're reacting just the way he wants us to."

"What if it's Donahoe and not Cole doing it?" lisped Povich between puffs on his pipe.

"What difference does it make?" demanded Craston. "The result is still the same. We're playing right into Cole's hands."

"I'm not so sure," said Stramm, who had been staring meditatively out the huge window into the darkness beyond.

"But everything fits!" protested Drake.

"Not necessarily," said Stramm. "First of all, it fits only if you grant Cole the power to forsee the course of this meeting, or to control our minds. I'm not at all convinced he possesses either power; if he did, they would have been evident long before now. Even granting that, it fits only if every word Donahoe told us was a lie and every torture we inflicted upon him was done with his or Cole's consent. I don't accept that, either. As I said earlier, I fully believe he is telling the truth when he says he wants to kill Gareth Cole."

"And even if Donahoe himself possesses powers comparable to Cole's," continued Stramm, watching the others for their reactions, "I still think your conclusion is faulty. Don't forget: we've seen Donahoe make some pretty bad blunders in the field, blunders that could easily have cost him his life. We've captured a handful of his soldiers from time to time, and learned that their opinion of his mentality and ability is amazingly low. And now we've observed him at close range for the past day, and his behavior seems to bear out everything we've previously known about him. Whatever powers he might possess, the power of subtlety is conspicuous by its absence.

"Therefore, I think we might be justified in taking the situation at face value. We have, in a prison cell beneath this room, a man who loathes Gareth Cole at least as much as he hates us, who has not presented enough of a threat to Cole for Cole to do away with him as yet, and who may well be willing to come over to our side."

"Then do you suggest turning him free, as Gerald does?" demanded Drake hotly.

"Within limits, yes," replied Stramm. "Gerald proposed, as I understand it, that we turn him completely loose and spy on his movements, primarily to see whether he returns to do battle with us or goes back to fight Gareth Cole."

"That's the gist of it," agreed Rysler. "Though I'd like to add that my prime reason for this suggestion was the appearance of Cole's creature last night. It seemed pretty obvious that Cole will make no attempt to protect or free Donahoe. Obviously he wants him dead; if so, I want him alive."

"And I'm betting that's just what Cole expected you to say," said Craston dryly.

"I'm betting it isn't," countered Stramm. "But be that as it may, I still find Gerald's plan to be unsuitable."

"Then you *are* on our side!" shouted Drake triumphantly.

"No, Michael, I'm not. I'd like to point out my objections to Gerald's proposition, just as I did to yours, and offer an idea or two of my own."

Drake stared angrily at him, but said nothing.

"I think the prime failing of Gerald's plan," continued Stramm, "is that nothing will have been gained by our capture of Donahoe. If he turns around and attacks us again, we'll have to try to capture him again—and

38

this time we may not be so fortunate. If, on the other hand, he returns to Cole, there are two possibilities.

"The first is that he was here as an agent for Cole. If so, he can now identify Michael, Gerald and myself as Barons, and he probably has a pretty good knowledge of the countryside.

"The second possibility is that he will return to do battle with Cole. If so, he will lose, for Cole undoubtedly has had the power to kill him many times over during the past day or two. And if he loses, we shall have gained nothing. Incidentally, I think you can forget about spying on him; if he returns to Cole, our men won't be able to follow him, and we'll know nothing of what happens.

"I think Michael and Andrew are equally wrong. I see absolutely no benefit to be gained from killing him."

"Are you serious?" exploded Drake incredulously.

"Yes," replied Stramm. "If he truly has powers that make him a rival to Cole, we won't be able to kill him. Agreed?" There was a general nodding of heads. "At best, such an attempt will cost us a few lives. If, on the other hand, he *can* be killed, then he has no such powers, and all we will have done is kill a general who might have given us considerable strategic information had we allowed him to live."

"Now that you've managed to puncture holes in all of our plans and options," wheezed Povich, coughing out great gobs of dark gray smoke, "perhaps you'd like to tell us what you have in mind."

"Gladly, Aldan," said Stramm, rising to his feet and leaning his hands on the ancient table.

When he had finished, Drake jumped up in a rage. "Elston," he yelled, his voice reverberating through the large room, "if your motives weren't above reproach, I'd call that treason!"

"I'll call it treason anyway," said Craston in a cold, level voice.

"Consider the advantages," said Stramm calmly. "Regardless of what Donahoe is and what he wants, it will get us inside Cole's headquarters."

"To be slaughtered!" shouted Drake.

"If so, then we'll be slaughtered a hell of a lot closer to our goal than we've ever been before. Aren't you a little tired of seeing generation after generation of our men dying on the beaches?"

"At least they have a chance there," shot back Drake. "What you're suggesting is utter suicide!"

"Perhaps not," said Rysler. "If Donahoe is telling the truth, there's every reason to believe that Elston's reasoning is valid. And even if Donahoe *does* have some powers we don't know about, there's still an excellent chance he'll use them the way we want him to."

"I say it's lunacy!" insisted Drake. "And I'm not going to let my army be a part of it!"

"Well, that's that," shrugged Povich, tapping his pipe idly against the arm of his chair. "We act together or not at all."

"Just a minute," said Rysler. "I think Elston's plan is the only one that makes any sense—and that includes my own. Let Michael stay home and sulk if he wants to, but I'm going through with it, even if I have to do it alone."

"Count me out," said Craston. "If I'm going to commit treason, I'll do it with some personal gain in mind. I say kill him, and the sooner the better."

"Let's put it to a vote," suggested Rysler.

All eyes turned to Povich. The old man with the gentle lisp and huge, burly body would be the tie-breaker. He looked nervously around the table, then fumbled once more with his pipe, singeing his fingers in the process.

A moment later Michael Drake and Andrew Craston stalked furiously out of the room, and unanimity among the Council of Barons was lost forever.

40

Donahoe chafed in his bonds. His shoulder had begun to stiffen again. An insect, large and wet, crawled up the side of his cot and began climbing across his chest, only to become lost in his beard. He could feel it at the newly opened cuts on his throat; he didn't know what it was doing there, but it hurt like Rath. With a grunt, he managed to turn partially onto his side, but was unable to dislodge the insect. Having failed to do so, he tried to ignore it and glared balefully at the moist stone ceiling.

Suddenly he brought his chin down hard against his chest, and allowed himself a triumphant grin as he felt the body of the insect crack and turn into pulp in the folds of his neck. He lay back again, more relaxed, and stared almost hypnotically at the tiny trickle of water that ran down the wall a few feet from his head.

He had been alone for more than a day, with neither food nor water. His hands and feet were still bound to the cot. Many times he had considered begging Gareth for help; each time he had rejected the idea, growing more and more furious as the hours passed. It would be just like Gareth to let him rot here in this dank hole until he was good and penitent. Well, it wouldn't work! He could take anything the Normans could hand out, and more. Sooner or later they would untie him, of that he was sure. After all, if they had wanted to kill him, they would have done so long before this.

Or would they? Were they waiting to see if Gareth would rescue him, if Gareth *could* rescue him from this great a distance?

No, that wouldn't be it. Gareth had already proved

he could send his creatures inside the dungeon if he wished.

Certainly they weren't trying to frighten him. They'd seen him in battle all too often to believe that Red Will Donahoe was afraid of anything. And if this was the Norman idea of torture, they had a lot to learn about their art.

So it wasn't torture, it wasn't to induce fear, and it wasn't to test Gareth Cole's powers. And even had he possessed the faintest degree of modesty, which he did not, it would have been inconceivable to him that they had forgotten so notorious a captive.

Which brought him, in his slovenly mental trek, back to the original question: what were they waiting for?

Wait a minute! Wait a minute. They had said something, Stramm and Michael Drake and even Rysler. What was the word? *Mutant!* Gareth had used it too. And someone, one of the Normans, wanted to know about his powers, as if he were one of Gareth's band of freaks.

Yes, that had to be it! But here he was stymied, for he did not know the meaning of the word mutant. From the way Drake and the others had used it, he had assumed it to be an insult—but if Gareth used it too, even called himself one, then it had to mean something else, something far more significant.

Was it good or bad? He didn't know, though he hoped it was bad, for Gareth had called him a mutant in reverse, and Gareth was never wrong. The thought of Cole standing smug and untouchable in the tunnels, listening in on his thoughts and laughing at them, brought back the bloodlust. His reasoning processes, fragile at best, ceased operating altogether and he tugged blindly at his bonds, bellowing like a bull.

How long he kept it up, he didn't know; but finally the door opened and Stramm and Rysler returned.

"Still here, I see," commented Stramm.

"What did you expect?" demanded Donahoe, panting from his exertions.

"I had no idea what to expect," came the reply. "That's why I left you like this."

"And now what?" said the redbeard.

"Now I have a little proposition to offer you," said Stramm.

"I don't make deals with Normans!"

"Wait until you've heard it—and the word is Normal. How would you like your freedom?"

"Hah!"

"I mean it. In fact, I'm going to begin by untying you right now. Rysler will have you covered with a poison-tipped arrow, so I wouldn't try anything rash if I were you."

Rysler stepped back and fitted an arrow to his bow while Stramm severed the redbeard's bonds with his sword. Donahoe swung his legs to the ground and began massaging his wrists. His eyes fell on Stramm and he stood up ominously.

"Careful," said Rysler softly, simultaneously drawing back the bowstring. Donahoe turned to him, frowned, and sat down again.

"That's better," said Stramm. "And now to business. I take it you feel no great affection for Gareth Cole."

"I'd like to rip his head off his body and cut his heart out—and someday I will!" vowed the redbeard.

"How would you like the chance?" said Stramm softly.

"What are you getting at?" said the redbeard, staring at the other's satanic features.

"I'll put it this way," began Stramm. "None of our people has ever been to Cole's headquarters—at least, none has ever been there and back."

"You're damned right they haven't!" said the redbeard proudly.

"You, on the other hand, probably know the subways as well as anyone except Gareth Cole."

"Subways?"

"Where you live."

"You mean the tunnels?"

"Yes, the tunnels. We don't know what Gareth Cole can do, at least not the whole of it. And even if you don't know the limit of his powers, you certainly are more acquainted with them than we are."

"What are you getting at?" repeated Donahoe.

"You hate Gareth Cole, don't you?" asked Stramm.

"Yes."

"More than you hate anything or anyone else?"

"Yes!"

"Enough to lead an army against him?"

Donahoe let out a low whistle and stared dumbly at Stramm. He scratched his shaggy head, whistled again, and threw back his head and laughed.

"Let me get this straight. You want me to . . ."

". . . lead an attack upon Gareth Cole's stronghold."

"You must be joking!"

"If there's one thing I never joke about, it's Gareth Cole."

"How do you know I won't lead them into a trap?"

"I don't know now—but I'll know before you're entrusted with the army."

"This is like some kind of crazy dream!" said the redbeard, more to himself than to Stramm. "Imagine—Red Will Donahoe leading a raid against the tunnels!" He laughed again.

"Think about it," said Stramm.

And Donahoe did. He thought about the feel of Gareth Cole's white throat in his hands, thought of shaking the tiny body until its brain came loose and splattered against the top of its cranium, thought of Gareth Cole's head hanging from his belt, attached with a lock of pale blond hair. And he thought of himself at the head of an army that needed speech to transmit information, that could only advance by marching, that felt pain

44

when a sword or arrow found its mark. Both were pleasant pictures. Then he thought of Gareth Cole watching him as he spoke with Stramm, laughing to himself as the redbeard plotted his death.

"I'll do it!" bellowed the redbeard. Rysler jumped at the suddenness with which the silence had been broken.

"Good," said Stramm. "I suppose we'd better get down to the details."

"When can I start?" interrupted Donahoe.

"When I feel I can trust you," replied Stramm. "And when my men will follow you. Not for a month or two, I should say. It'll take them at least that long to adjust to the idea of being led by a mutant, even one that didn't work out."

"What are you talking about?" demanded Donahoe.

"Surely you must have guessed by now, even if you didn't already know," said Stramm.

"I don't know anything."

"I can see you're due for a bit of a history lesson," said Stramm, seating himself at the far end of the cot.

"History?"

"Yes, history—as much as of it as we can reassemble. Almost a thousand years ago there was a war, a pretty bad one. I gather it didn't last very long. We have no idea what weapons they used, but evidently they were enough to destroy almost everything on the face of the earth."

"Earth?" repeated Donahoe dumbly.

"The world . . . what we live on. Never mind. Just believe me: almost everyone was killed. Entire civilizations were obliterated in the space of a few hours, if the few records we have of that conflict are accurate. Frankly, I can't conceive of anything being that powerful, but I guess it doesn't make much difference whether it took hours or years. The fact remains that it was accomplished. Every man, or almost every man, on the surface of the planet was killed."

"That's a bunch of crap," exploded the redbeard. "If that were true, we wouldn't be here!"

"You're getting ahead of me," said Stramm. "As I was saying, every man on the surface of the planet was killed; whether quickly or slowly, it makes no difference. However, not everyone was *on* the surface; some, a veritable handful compared to the billions who died, were *under* it."

"What?"

"Under it," repeated Stramm. "The war, it would seem, was not totally unexpected. Many people were able to hide in caves and something called bomb shelters. These people waited a number of years before coming out from concealment, and formed the basis of our current civilization."

"What does that have to do with Gareth—or with me?" asked the redbeard, not at all sure he wasn't being duped with some far-fetched fairy tale.

"I'm coming to that," said Stramm patiently. "You see, there was one other place beneath the ground that offered some shelter: the subway systems."

"What in Rath are subways?"

"It's hard to explain, possibly because we ourselves aren't too clear on the subject. As far as we can tell, it was a system of underground transportation. Trains—a type of vehicle—carried people from one place to another via underground tunnels."

"The tunnels!" exclaimed Donahoe, forgetting his skepticism. "The tunnels are the subways!"

"Correct. And it was in the subways that another group of people hid to escape the ravages of the war. Unfortunately, they didn't totally succeed. I don't know what kind of weapons were used, but it seems clear that once they were put into play, even the air was unfit for survival. And while the caves and shelters supplied their own air and could be completely cut off from the outside world, the subways could not. There were too many entrances and exits, too many ventilation shafts, to effectively keep this poisoned air entirely out of the system. The air had a strange effect upon the survivors. In a word, it caused considerable genetic damage that ultimately resulted in a number of unpredictable mutations."

"That word again!" growled the redbeard. "What is a mutation?"

"A freak of nature. A man who is somehow different from his parents and his companions. Originally the mutants were put to death, since they were easily spotted—you know, three heads, no eyes, and the like. The people in the tunnels, as you call them, remained there, having no desire to affect any normal survivors who might have come back out onto the surface. And, after a few generations, they thought they *had* gotten rid of all the mutants.

"They were wrong.

"You see, they had no way of identifying a mutant who was normal in physical appearance. But eventually, one was born."

"Gareth Cole!" exclaimed Donahoe.

"Right. For years he seemed no different from any of the others, except perhaps to be a bit more sickly. From what we can reconstruct, his powers came to him slowly; even *he* didn't realize what he was until he was perhaps thirty years old, though he might have had an inkling, since he seems to have stopped aging at twenty-five or so.

"He was born in the ruins of a city called Chicago, and after he had reached the full maturity of his powers, he left his home to go out and seek others like himself. He found none.

"The subways of New York—your tunnels—were the last system he checked. It was there that he decided to set up his headquarters, and in the process he drove all the residents of the subway—my ancestors—out.

47

"They came at last to the ruins of a somewhat circular city, which a few other survivors had already taken over. It was called the Hub, possibly because of its structure. We have since learned that it was originally known as Boston.

"We began life anew, staking out claims on the land. It has passed from father to son for centuries. Occasionally we made raids on other Normal cities, taking prisoners and setting them to work in the fields.

"From time to time Gareth—or, to be more precise, monsters from whatever hell Gareth has made a pact with—appeared and stole some of our women. It wasn't until a hundred years ago that we realized what he was doing with them."

"And what was that?"

"He was using them for breeding stock."

Donahoe looked puzzled.

"Don't you understand?" said Stramm. "*He was trying to breed an army of mutants!*"

"He's succeeded," grunted the redbeard.

"I think not," replied Stramm. "Or else why hasn't he destroyed us? We began our war with him when we finally discovered what he was up to. If he has done what he set out to do, why hasn't he overrun the world with his mutated armies?"

"He doesn't need them," said Donahoe, admitting the fact reluctantly. "He could destroy the Hub in two seconds if he felt like it."

"Then why doesn't he?" demanded Rysler sharply.

"He doesn't care about you," replied the redbeard.

"He doesn't care about us?" repeated Rysler unbelievingly. "Then why does he send his armies against us?"

"If he wanted to destroy the Hub, he'd do it himself."

"You didn't answer my question," said Rysler.

"I don't know the answer," said Donahoe.

"Then let's try another question," said Stramm. "What is *your* power?"

"I don't have any."

"Then why do you lead his forces?"

"I'm the best man he has." He paused to consider the remark, then amended it. "I'm the *only* man he has."

"Why didn't he drive you out, as he did the other Normals?" persisted Stramm.

"I'm no Norman!" thundered the redbeard.

"Well, you're no mutant either," said Stramm. "So just what are you?"

"I'm Red Will Donahoe!" he cried, half in rage and half in agony. "That's what I am! I'm Red Will Donahoe, and I'm nobody's damned pawn! Not yours, not Gareth's, not anyone's! I came here to kill Normans because *I* wanted to, and if I lead your army against Gareth Cole, it'll be my decision, not yours!"

"Nobody's saying otherwise," said Stramm calmly. "We're just trying to figure out why Cole keeps a sport like you around."

"A sport?"

"A freak, if you will."

"*I'm* no freak!" roared the redbeard.

"To Cole and his mutants you are," said Stramm. "You're as much of an outsider to them as Cole would be to us. And yet he's given you command of his fighting forces. Why? Do you know something that could hurt him if he were to drive you out?"

"No."

"Besides," added Rysler, "if he were that dangerous, Cole would have killed him."

"True," agreed Stramm. "We'll simply have to approach it from the other direction: if we don't know how you can harm Cole, let's figure out how you can help us. What do you know about the tunnels?"

"I know every inch of them," said Donahoe.

"Does Cole?" asked Stramm. "No, forget that. Of course he does. Can you approach them undetected?"

"Not a chance," replied Donahoe.

"How large a force would you need to insure victory?"

"What's the use?" exploded the redbeard angrily. "He'd see us coming from miles away. Even a heavy fog won't hide the boats for long."

"Then we won't use boats," said Stramm.

"What do you expect me to do—swim?" asked Donahoe contemptuously.

"Have you ever heard of the Holland Tunnel?" asked Stramm.

"No."

"Have you ever followed one huge tunnel up to a wall of boulders?"

"Yes."

"That's the Holland Tunnel. We barricaded it more than a century ago to stop mutant raiding parties. Is it patrolled?"

"Not so you'd notice it."

"What does that mean?"

"Gareth doesn't need foot soldiers to see who's coming. He just knows. So do Jon and some of the others."

"Of course," said Stramm, drumming his fist against his other hand. "I should have known that."

"Then there's no way you can approach undetected?" asked Rysler.

"No way," repeated Donahoe.

"Which means Cole will be ready for you, no matter what precautions we take."

"That's what I've been trying to tell you," growled the redbeard.

"And if *he's* ready for you," continued Rysler, "his army will be ready for you."

"I can defeat his freaks," said Donahoe firmly.

"That's debatable," said Stramm, "but it's not the crux of the matter. The question is: can you defeat Gareth Cole?"

"Let me get my hands on him and—"

"Forget it, mutant!" snapped Stramm. "You've been trying to get your hands on him all your life, and I

50

can't see that it's done you a hell of a lot of good. If Cole enters the battle, and sooner or later he must, it will be with those infernal mental monsters of his. It's them you'll have to defeat."

"It's no use, Elston," said Rysler. "We've been trying for generations. Nothing can harm them."

Stramm glared at him for a moment. Then his expression softened, his shoulders sagged, and he spoke softly. "You're right, of course," he said.

"Like Rath he is!" hissed Donahoe.

"What?"

A picture of a firebird flashed through the redbeard's mind. A man—himself—stood on a blood-soaked beach, a newly severed head hanging from his belt. He picked up a rock and hurled it at the firebird—and the creature screamed in pain.

"Like Rath he is!" repeated Donahoe. "Give me a chance and I'll present you with a belt made of Gareth Cole's entrails!"

"You remembered something!" said Stramm excitedly. "What was it?"

"That's my passport out of this damned city," grinned the redbeard. "I'll tell you when I feel like it—*if* I feel like it!"

Stramm appeared to consider this for a moment. "All right, mutant. It looks like we'll have to trust each other."

"That we will," said Donahoe, getting to his feet and stretching. "And since I'm going to be here for a few weeks, I want a place to stay. Something secluded."

"Secluded?"

"Just for once, I don't want anyone staring at the inside of my head—or the outside."

"It'll be done," promised Stramm.

"And one more thing," said the redbeard, finally picking the squashed insect off his neck. "I'll be in no mood to train your army with an empty stomach—or an empty bed."

51

CHAPTER SEVEN

She was plain.

Her name was Alutha Drake, and while she was not quite ugly, she was far from pretty. It didn't matter much any more, though once it had so upset her that she was ashamed to look into a mirror.

That had been long ago, though, back before she had learned that when you were Andrew Povich's daughter no one mentioned your lack of beauty. And when she married Michael Drake to further unite the Council of Barons, no one dared mention it even behind her back, for Michael Drake was not quite as forgiving as her father had been.

There were a lot of things Drake wasn't forgiving about. Though it was hardly Alutha's fault, he still blamed her for the necessity of his political marriage, and had not touched her since their wedding night some four years past. He was none too happy with old Povich, either, partially because of the marriage and partially because Povich was the titular head of the Council of Barons. And, more recently, he had come to explode in a fit of rage at the mention of Elston Stramm's name. He blamed Stramm for keeping Donahoe alive and convincing Povich and Rysler to supply him with soldiers. And, since the proprieties had to be observed within the Council, he took out his anger on Alutha.

She was alone now, sitting in her bedchambers, absently brushing her long black hair. Once she had dreamed of her hair falling about her in long, flowing locks, but somehow it had remained curly and snarled into adulthood. Usually she wore it up, covering it with a shawl or a scarf; but in the privacy of her rooms, she let it fall down about her waist in the hope that enough brushing might somehow transform it into the crowning glory she had wished for long ago.

She glanced absently out of her window, down to the street below. It was empty as usual, for Drake never saw any reason to post a guard around his castle unless he was in it. He could conceive of no reason why anyone might want his wife, but he had made it as easy as possible for them to steal off with her if they were so inclined. As yet no one had cared to, somewhat to his disappointment.

Alutha thought of the cordoned-off section on the third level of the castle. She had never been there, but she knew as surely as she knew her own name that Drake kept a woman there. As a matter of fact, she was sure there was more than one. She didn't really blame him. After all, he had married her for a single purpose: to gain a barony. She had served that purpose, and he saw no further use in her. In earlier times she supposed he would have had her killed, but as long as Povich still held power, it was essential that he preserve her health, or at least give the appearance of so doing.

As for Alutha, she had long since become resigned to the situation. Once, many years ago, there had been a young man, a man with golden hair and a lean, hard body. She had never once spoken to him, for he was a mere warrior and she a Baron's daughter. Each day she had devised new ploys to see him as he patrolled her father's grounds, and one evening she had fallen into his arms, pretending to stumble in the darkened corridors. She blushed now as she thought of her shamelessness that evening, but a warm glow remained as she recalled the feel of his arms around her as he set her back on her feet. Then one day he had gone off to do battle against Gareth Cole, and she never saw him again. It was said that Donahoe carried his head around on a belt.

But she was young then, a lovesick girl. Now she was a woman, and with a sigh she went about her womanly duties, idly wondering if her husband might be returning soon, but not really caring.

Michael Drake's thoughts, at that moment, were far from home and hearth. Povich had called another meeting of the Council of Barons in a last-minute attempt to convince Drake and Craston to support Donahoe's campaign. Craston had refused outright to attend; Drake had agreed only on the condition that Donahoe be present to answer questions.

Three weeks had passed since they had captured him, weeks in which the redbeard had done very little except sate his various hungers. Finally, under Stramm's insistent prodding, he had gone about the business of training his army.

The process proved to be relatively simple. Since the tunnels were to be invaded, the number of men had to be held down to a manageable size: otherwise there would be no room for Donahoe to manipulate and deploy his forces. Stramm, Povich and Rysler each supplied him with two hundred soldiers. The redbeard lined them up, took one brief walk up and down the row of humanity, and declared himself ready to do battle. It was then that Povich called the meeting.

Drake arrived in the great hall of Povich's castle just as Stramm and Donahoe made their appearance. Rysler and the old man were waiting for them.

"Any word from Craston?" asked Stramm as he lowered himself to a window seat.

"None," replied Povich, lighting his ever-present pipe. "I'm afraid he really isn't going to show up."

"No great loss," said the redbeard, half-sitting, half-sprawling on a large wooden chair. "In fact, I don't know why you dragged this one into it," he added, indicating Drake with a contemptuous thumb.

"Watch your tongue, mutant!" snapped Drake.

Donahoe laughed at him and reached for a goblet of wine. He drained it, wiped a few stray drops from his beard, and turned to Povich. "What's this all about, anyway?" he demanded suddenly.

"It's about your forthcoming confrontation with Gareth Cole," replied Povich.

"We're ready," grunted the redbeard.

"Fine," replied Rysler. "When will you begin training them?"

"Train them? We're ready to fight right now!" was the response.

"But surely you have some strategy mapped out!" protested Povich, lisping more noticeably than usual. "Surely you don't intend merely to invade the subways and hope for the best!"

"Yes, I have a strategy," said Donahoe calmly. "My strategy is to kill Gareth Cole."

"That's all there is to it?" asked Povich unbelievingly.

"That's all you have to know," said the redbeard, walking over to Stramm and taking his wine from him.

"Elston," said the oldest Baron, "I think we had better discuss this in greater detail. When I voted with you and Gerald, I was under the impression that we would be told the plan of attack, and would be able to make suggestions and improvements."

"Nobody gives me orders!" said Donahoe emphatically.

"Nobody is trying to," said Rysler patiently. "All we want to know is how you intend to defeat Cole."

"And two seconds after I told you, Drake would put an arrow through my heart," replied Donahoe.

"How do you know I won't anyway?" said Drake, speaking for the first time.

"First of all," said the redbeard, "no one else knows how to fight Gareth Cole. And second, you haven't enough guts to kill a fly."

Drake reddened and placed his hand to the hilt of his sword.

"Pull it out and it's the last sword you'll ever draw!" snarled the redbeard, glaring at him from halfway across the room.

"Watch your tongue, mutant!" snapped Drake, his hand not moving.

"To Rath with you!"

"Come now, Michael," said Povich. "Don't let him upset you. It's just his manner of speaking."

"Then he needs a lesson in manners," said Drake.

"If I ever get one," bellowed Donahoe, "it won't be from a man who hasn't got the stomach to fight Gareth Cole!"

Stramm had been watching Donahoe and Drake intently, planning to interject himself into the argument if tempers got out of hand. He decided that the moment had come and he strode over to Donahoe, intending to take the redbeard's arm and lead him away from Drake.

A moment later he lay flat on his back, tasting warm, salty blood where three of his teeth should have been.

"Keep out of this, Norman!" yelled Donahoe.

"Somebody give him a sword," said Drake, finally unsheathing his own.

"I don't need any weapons against a Norman!". bellowed Donahoe.

"I seem to remember you saying that once before, mutant," replied Drake, a cold smile on his lips.

The redbeard lowered his head and charged the young Baron like a bull. Drake sidestepped him, reached out with his sword and hooked it around Donahoe's arm. The redbeard felt the keen edge of steel bite into his skin. He pulled against it, felt a sudden bolt of pain throughout the length of his arm, and then the sword flew out of Drake's grasp and clattered noisily to the ground.

Donahoe turned back to Drake, mouthing a steady

stream of curses. He reached out a huge hand, grabbed the Baron by the throat, lifted him completely off the ground, and drove his other hand into Drake's face. When he removed it, nothing remained of Drake's nose except a shapeless mass of bloody cartilege.

Drake struggled vainly to free himself from Donahoe's grip. The redbeard released him for an instant, then encircled his body with massive arms and locked his hands together. Drake flailed his arms weakly, then suddenly went rigid. There was a loud cracking noise, and Donahoe hurled the corpse onto the floor with a grunt of disgust. Even the spasmodic twitching of death was absent from the grotesquely twisted body.

The redbeard glared defiantly at the remaining Barons, prepared for a mass attack. Povich and Rysler just stared mutely at what had so recently been Michael Drake, but Stramm was back on his feet, sword in hand.

"I would advise you to stand right where you are," he said to Donahoe. "I can promise you that I will not prove quite so easy an adversary."

Somehow Donahoe knew he was telling the truth, that Stramm would be a difficult man to defeat even if the redbeard were armed. He did as Stramm told him, tensed and ready for whatever might happen next.

"Well, gentlemen," said Stramm, never taking his eyes from Donahoe, "we seem to have been presented with still another problem."

"I say kill him!" said Rysler hotly. "Andrew and Michael were right—we should have destroyed him the moment we first captured him!"

"Nonsense!" said Stramm sharply. "He is still our only hope against Gareth Cole. And in case you've forgotten, Michael drew his weapon first. The mutant was unarmed throughout the battle."

"True," said Povich reluctantly. "But do you realize what this means, Elston?"

"It's possible," replied Stramm. "But I suggest that we withhold judgment until we return from the subways. Then we can decide upon it."

"Decide on what?" demanded the redbeard.

"You've placed us in an awkward position," said Stramm. "According to our law, any man who kills a childless Baron in a fair fight receives the spoils of battle."

"What does that mean?"

"It means you could conceivably take over his position and all his possessions. However, your status is at best uncertain." He paused, then turned to Rysler and Povich. "I move that we see how he comports himself in the war against Cole before we reach a ruling on his case."

"Agreed," said Povich. Then, turning to Donahoe, he added, "But you really didn't have to kill him."

"I didn't hear anyone telling him not to kill *me!*" snapped the redbeard. He stepped over the corpse as if it weren't there and sought out another wine goblet. Suddenly he grinned. "So I own everything he did! Did he have a wife?"

"Shut up!" said Stramm irritably.

"I'll see to her after I've taken care of Gareth," said Donahoe.

"What shall we do about Michael?" asked Rysler, staring at the twisted body as if hypnotized.

"Let him rot, for all I give a damn," said the redbeard, draining his goblet and walking out into the afternoon sun.

CHAPTER EIGHT

It was a dull funeral. Long and dull and filled with considerable pomp and ceremony. One by one each Baron spoke over the grave; all but Rysler were eloquent, and Povich was interminable. Donahoe had either the gall or the ignorance to attend, and Stramm kept a watchful eye on him at all times, lest there be a repeat performance and another job for the gravediggers.

Povich spoke to his son-in-law's mourners for three hours, and might easily have doubled or even trebled that amount of time had not a merciful Nature elected to give a display of thunder, lightning and rain that ultimately silenced the old man and sent the mourners scurrying to the warmth and safety of their homes.

The redbeard accompanied the three united Barons—Craston had departed the moment he was finished speaking—to Povich's castle. Even his untutored barbaric eye was dazzled by the brilliant array of foliage surrounding the oldest Baron's magnificent estate. Everywhere he looked he found colorful displays of flowers of every imaginable shape and color. A score of carefully laid stone paths wound in and out among them, occasionally obscured by huge flowering bushes, now and then covered with exotic mosses and ivies, glistening from the recent rains.

The interior of the castle boasted a quiet splendor of its own, on the surface similar to Rysler's palatial dwelling, but on closer inspection quite unique and distinctive. Simplicity was the hallmark of the building and its furnishings, just as it was the hallmark of Povich himself. The outsized furniture, though carefully hand-carved from the finest woods, was built primarily for comfort. No single piece stood out from the rest, not even the forty-foot table in the massive dining hall. Povich was the only Baron besides Craston to have hooked up an intricate indoor plumbing system, and each room was equipped with its own bath and lavatory. There were murals on the sturdy timbers that formed the walls, but only a handful depicted the Normals in battles. Most were pastoral scenes and landscapes, and a goodly number seemed to have been taken from Povich's gardens. Even the servants added to the atmosphere of the old house. Stramm kept no servants, Drake's were all warriors, and Craston's were never seen. Only Rysler and Povich had servants who lived up to their names, and Rysler's always seemed more to be wage-earners than devoted chattels; just the opposite impression was given by the men and women who scurried hither and thither about the dwelling of Aldan Povich.

They stopped at the library, a huge room filled from floor to ceiling with bookshelves and cases, though in fact it contained no more than fifty books at best. Literature was always at a premium, and since only Stramm and Craston displayed any real interest in it, Povich and the others felt no discomfort over their massive but empty book rooms.

"Which one was his widow?" asked the redbeard as soon as Povich's personal attendant had closed the door behind them.

"No one demands that you be in good taste, mutant," said Stramm disgustedly, "but you might at least have the courtesy to keep your mouth shut until Drake's body is properly cold."

"It's not Drake's cold body I'm concerned with," guffawed Donahoe. "It's his wife's hot one!"

"One more remark like that and I'll have at you myself!" snapped Rysler.

"Just try it," said Donahoe ominously.

"Shut up, mutant!" said Stramm. "I didn't keep you alive to kill Normals. Save your bloodlust for Gareth Cole; you'll probably need it and everything else you have, just to make him work up a good sweat before he kills you."

Stramm's words had the proper effect on the redbeard, as he had known they would. Donahoe immediately fell silent, staring intently at his hands as he clenched and unclenched them. The mere mention of Cole's name seemed to drive him into untold depths of rage, and Stramm used his awareness of that fact whenever he felt it expedient. It always worked.

"Speaking of killing Cole," said Povich, lighting his pipe, "this might be the proper time for a reassessment of our situation."

"As you wish," shrugged Stramm.

"You still want to proceed with the invasion of the subways, I take it?"

"Of course. Michael's death changes nothing."

"Changes nothing?" repeated Povich incredulously. "For God's sake, Elston, you're asking us to hand our finest soldiers over to a man who has killed a Baron!"

"To be perfectly truthful, Michael asked for it. I wish he were still alive, but he had it coming to him."

"You're damned right he did!" said the redbeard without looking up.

"But Elston . . ."

"Listen, Aldan," said Stramm. "The success or failure of this raid depends upon Donahoe's ability to pierce through Cole's physical and mental defenses and destroy him. I can't see that Michael's death makes our chances of success any greater or lesser. If Donahoe could lead a successful invasion a week ago, he still can; and if he couldn't do it then, I doubt that Michael's death has increased his ability to kill Cole."

"I know all this," protested Povich. "It's just that I don't think our men will follow him into the subways.

It was doubtful before, and now that he's killed Michael, I'd say it was almost a certainty."

"We'll go with him," said Stramm. "Surely your men will follow you."

"I suppose so," said Povich dubiously.

"Well, I can guarantee that mine will follow me," said Rysler.

"Just so long as they take their orders from me, I don't care whom they follow," interjected the redbeard.

"We'll see about that," said Rysler.

"I promise that they'll follow any reasonable command you give," said Stramm. "If your idea of a reasonable command differs considerably from ours, we'll just have to improvise."

"Do you think we should make another attempt to get Andrew to join us?" asked the old man between puffs on his pipe.

"Fat lot of good it'll do," said Rysler, walking over to a small row of books and absently thumbing his way through one of them.

"I'm inclined to agree with Gerald," said Stramm. "I very much doubt that Andrew would consider coming with us."

"Who needs a blind man anyway?" demanded Donahoe. "He'd only be in the way."

"What we need is a symbol of Baronal unity," said Povich irritably, "though I don't imagine someone like you could understand."

Donahoe glared at the old man but said nothing. When it became obvious that the ensuing silence was not going to be soon broken, he turned his back on the Barons and began pacing up and down the inlaid wooden floor. It helped to ease his tension, for he was in every way a sensualist, and his senses told him that this was the quickest way to relax his tautened nerves and muscles. He took a deep breath. The room smelled of the many woods which comprised it, and he was glad that, much as Povich loved his flowers, he left them out in the garden where they belonged. He strode by the three men once again, then walked over to a window and looked out. Flowers were not exactly a rarity to him, but since none grew in the tunnels, he saw them only when he was making war. He liked the feeling he had within him as the plethora of vivid colors assailed his eyes. They evoked no sense of wonder at their beauty, but simply a childlike satisfaction that he had found a number of pretty objects to hold his attention. At last he tired of looking at them and turned back to the Barons. Rysler was studiously thumbing through the pages of another book, Povich was busying himself with his pipe, which seemed to continually be dying on him, and Stramm was staring curiously in his direction.

"If you're quite through with your tantrum," said Stramm, "perhaps you'd like to accompany me back to my castle for dinner."

"Dinner?" repeated the redbeard. "Is it that late?"

"Are you hungry?"

"Yes."

"Then what's the difference? Besides, I don't believe our discussion is likely to continue toward any fruitful conclusion."

"Will you at least speak to Andrew once more?" asked Povich.

"Why me?" replied Stramm. "He and I are not exactly the closest of companions. In fact, I would go so far as to say that we bear quite a cordial distaste for one another."

"That's just the point of it," said Povich. "If you go, he'll know it's not simply a gesture, but a serious invitation to patch up our differences."

"All right," sighed Stramm. "Not that I'll accomplish anything, but I'll do it as a personal favor to you, Aldan."

He and Donahoe took their leave and began the six-mile trek to Stramm's castle. Most of the time the other

Barons either rode horses (or, rather, the peculiar animals that horses had become) or hired out the Hub's version of a rickshaw for visits between their estates; but Stramm preferred walking, and in Donahoe he had found the perfect companion for that avocation, if for nothing else.

They strode down the long road in silence. Occasionally a broken slab of concrete stuck up through the dirt surface, but for the most part it was no different from the numerous little backroads that circled Stramm's grounds. They passed no residences on the way, since all the Barons but Craston lived on the outskirts of the Hub, but here and there they could see signs of ancient dwellings: a foundation, an ancient sewer, and just beyond Povich's boundaries a single stone fireplace and chimney, the sole remnant of a home that had existed eleven hundred years before.

After they had walked about three miles, Donahoe turned to his companion and said suddenly: "Why in Rath is everyone so concerned about a blind man?"

"I hope that hasn't been bothering you all this time," Stramm smiled.

"You didn't answer my question."

"No, I didn't, did I? Well, as you know, Andrew is a Baron. We have no single man in command here, as you seem to have in Gareth Cole, or as Springfield has in its Lord Chancellor. The five Barons—four, now—have always ruled jointly. It's a good thing in many ways, for it stops any one man from acquiring too much power and abusing it. Not that we don't all try for that power, mind you, but it seems unlikely that any one of us shall succeed in gaining it."

"What's to stop the man with the most powerful army from taking anything he wants?" asked the redbeard.

"A most logical question. You amaze me, mutant." Stramm paused, then continued. "The basis of our political stand-off is our method of recruiting our armies. Each of us is free to draft every fifth man for a period of three years, during which time we must both pay him and support his dependents. Naturally, we each draft every man we can to make absolutely certain no army is stronger than our own."

"But one general can make the difference in a battle," protested Donahoe. "I've proved it many times!"

"In a relatively even battle, yes. But there has always been an odd number of Barons in power. Occasionally there have been only three, and once there were seven. Numbers are unimportant. The fact remains that with an odd number of Barons, no battle is ever so close that a single general can turn the tide."

"What's to stop you from attacking, say, Rysler? That would make it an even fight."

"An even fight couldn't be tolerated. Whoever won would doubtless assimilate the loser's army and property, and then it's conceivable that he couldn't be stopped. Therefore, Andrew and Aldan would have to choose sides the moment the battle began."

"And if they each chose a different side?"

"Then Drake's army would be the deciding factor. And whichever side it chose, that side would win. This would reduce the number of Barons to three, assuming you or somebody else takes over Michael's title in time, and again you would have a situation in which no man could defeat the other two."

"What's to stop two of them from banding together to remove the third?" queried the redbeard.

"The knowledge that it wouldn't be worth the risk. Neither would gain absolute power by the maneuver, but the less adroit political and military manipulator of the pair would now stand to lose everything he had to his co-conspirator. It may seem too simple to be practical, and certainly there would seem to be a few inher-

65

ent weaknesses in the setup, but it's worked for a thousand years or so, and pragmatism is the ultimate test of any system."

"Interesting," said Donahoe, who was in fact totally bored with the entire matter. "What does it have to do with Craston?"

"I suppose I did digress a bit. I apologize. Anyway, it is imperative that we act as one whenever possible. The system I just described seems to work, but that doesn't mean that it hasn't been severely tested, and proved with the blood of countless thousands of warriors. You see, it doesn't allow the lust for power to succeed, but on the other hand, it doesn't stop people from trying."

"I don't follow."

"What I'm trying to say is that for as long as the battle takes, Andrew Craston will be the only Baron in the Hub. He will have complete control over its laws, its commerce, and its people—and its people just happen to include the bulk of our armies."

"Are you trying to say that you and Povich think he'll try to take over while we're fighting Gareth?" demanded the redbeard.

"It's quite possible. He might even succeed, especially if we're gone long enough for our men to start considering the possibility that Cole has beaten us. And even if he doesn't try, his refusal to give us even token support will tend to create serious divisions among our people. There will be various factions favoring each of us, and if they grow strong enough, it could draw us all into a civil war nobody wanted in the first place." He paused, satisfied. If anyone ever asked Donahoe about it, the redbeard would give the proper answers.

"Then you'd better put a little pressure on him," suggested Donahoe. "I'll lend a helping hand if you want."

"You mean a helping fist, don't you?"

"Whatever it takes," was the reply.

"I should have thought that even you would stop short of applying physical force to a blind man," said Stramm.

"I've got a lot at stake.

"You mean with Cole? I thought you told me you could accomplish it with a few hundred men."

"I can," said Donahoe. "But I'm a Baron now, just the same as you are. And I want to make sure my castle and my army and my woman are there when I get back."

"The trick is in getting back at all," pointed out Stramm. "I'd suggest that you apply all your mental gymnastics to that problem."

"Don't you worry about that!" snapped Donahoe. "When I get my hands on Gareth . . ."

"Yes, I know," interrupted Stramm. "You'll choke the life out of him, or whatever. Nonetheless, you're going to have to get your hands on him first."

"I'll do my part! You just see to it that Craston comes along!"

"I'll do my best," said Stramm, marveling at the fact that he could lie with such conviction.

CHAPTER NINE

The room was cold and dark, and Stramm had some difficulty finding his way to a chair. He'd been here before, when it was better lit, and he knew that Craston had thrown the room into shadows to annoy him. As his eyes adjusted themselves to the near-absence of light, he noted, with some amusement, long rows of ancient books stacked against the walls. The lack of dust on them implied that the blind Baron kept one or more of his servants pretty busy reading aloud to him each evening.

Stramm leaned back and stretched. He hadn't expected Craston to be waiting here for him; the man was too much of a politician for that. He would wait until Stramm started getting restless, and would try to time his entrance just before Stramm's temper broke and flared. Stramm smiled; this, at least, was nothing new. Since that bygone day when one of Cole's firebirds had blinded Craston, the youngest of the Barons had devoted his entire life to the politics of the Hub. Power politics, to be sure, but carried off neatly and effectively. Craston had always been intelligent, and the loss of his vision seemed to heighten his powers of mental deduction still further. Perhaps he had nothing else to do in his sunless world, reflected Stramm; but whatever the reason, Andrew Craston had honed his intellect and his instincts to a keen razor edge.

Stramm couldn't repress a grin when he recalled the manner in which Craston had first exhibited his political acumen in the Council. He himself had tried to impress upon the other Barons the need for a tariff on various agricultural items imported from neighboring Normal cities, inasmuch as they were frequently undercutting the locals' prices. Craston, for reasons of his own—he probably owned a piece of the action—was against the tax. The other three Barons were undecided, but leaned toward Stramm's position, primarily because of Craston's youth and supposed inexperience. Craston recognized this fact a few minutes into the discussion, and seemingly allowed himself to be swayed by Stramm's arguments, ultimately discoursing passionately and illogically for Stramm's tariff. He left so many holes in his argument that when the vote came, Rysler, Povich and Drake all were against the tariff, and Stramm and Craston went along with them in the interest of Povich's much sought after unanimity. No one but Stramm realized that Craston had manipulated them precisely as he had wished to, and he knew that from that day onward the blind Baron would be his only worthy antagonist on the Council.

Stramm began to get restless, and decided to participate in Craston's little game of upmanship. Walking slowly around the room, he began moving chairs, glasses, tables, just enough to cause some degree of discomfort to the sightless Baron. Then, satisfied, he seated himself on a hard, wooden chair, folded his arms across his chest, and waited. Finally, after what he guessed to be half an hour, he heard footsteps approaching.

"Elston?" came Craston's voice from down a corridor.

"In here," said Stramm, starting to rise to greet his host, then thinking better of it and remaining seated instead.

"I'm sorry to have kept you waiting," said Craston, closing the door behind him. "What can I do for you?"

"Nothing," said Stramm, watching him as the blind Baron made his way to another chair.

"Nothing?" repeated Craston in bemused tones. "Now

why is it that I think you've come to once again try to enlist my army in your crazy scheme to attack the subways?"

"That's precisely why I'm here," admitted Stramm. "However, I hardly look upon it as your doing me a favor; on the contrary, I'm going out of my way to help you."

"I would be interested," said Craston, groping blindly for a bottle of liquor, "to hear how sacrificingly my army can possibly work to my advantage." He gave a grunt of satisfaction as his hands finally found the bottle. He then sought out a glass in the same manner, and filled it without spilling a drop.

"No one is asking you to sacrifice your army," began Stramm patiently. "In fact, you need do nothing more than send along a two-hundred-man token of support."

"Token be damned!" snapped Craston. "Don't you think I know that no one is sending more than two hundred men?"

"What I meant," continued Stramm calmly, "is that your men, like ours, will hardly be enough to defeat Cole, if indeed he can be defeated. Our sole chance for success revolves around Donahoe and what he knows —or thinks he knows—of Cole's weaknesses."

"Then why send anyone at all?" demanded Craston. "Why not just send Donahoe in alone? Either he knows the answer or he doesn't; if he does, he won't need any help, and if he doesn't, twice as many soldiers won't do him a hell of a lot of good."

"I agree with you that the armies won't be worth a damn against Cole himself," said Stramm, "but if he sends out his mutants, then Donahoe will need all the protection we can furnish him until he's close enough to Cole to do whatever it is he has in mind."

"Have a drink, Elston," said Craston suddenly, pouring Stramm a tall glassful of liquor. "Is it good?"

"Yes. Very. What's it made of?"

"Fermented apples, disgusting as it may sound," grinned Craston. "Plus a bit of lemon peel and a few other odds and ends. I'm thinking of mass-producing it and going into business."

"You wouldn't be trying to change the subject, would you?" said Stramm, taking another sip of the concoction.

"Not at all," said Craston. "Actually, I was just making conversation until such time as you are willing to speak openly on the subject."

"I believe I was doing just that."

"Oh, come now, Elston," said the blind Baron irritably. "Shall we stop playing games?"

"Andrew Craston is forsaking subtlety?" said Stramm mockingly. "I can't believe it."

"Why did you really come here, Elston?" said Craston sharply.

"Because I told Aldan and Gerald I would make one last attempt to reunify the Council."

"I don't care what you told them. I want the truth."

"You're not making sense, Andrew."

"I think I am," said Craston, taking another sip from his crystalline glass. "Elston, let's put our cards on the table, shall we?"

"Go right ahead," said Stramm, his sprawling body giving no indication of the suddenly tense discipline he had applied to his mind.

"First of all, I'm not the least bit sorry that the mutant killed Michael Drake. He had it coming to him, and now there'll be that much more land and power for the rest of us."

"If Donahoe doesn't keep it for himself," interjected Stramm.

"He won't," said Craston. "I imagine you'll see to that, won't you, Elston? Surely you don't intend to let him live through the attack on Cole's headquarters?"

"To be perfectly honest about it, Andrew," said Stramm, "I don't think my intentions will make the slightest bit of difference. If he's wrong about being able to defeat Cole, I imagine Cole or the mutants will certainly dispose of him. If, on the other hand, he actually manages to kill Gareth Cole, then I very much doubt that our men could destroy him even if I ordered them to."

"Personally, I think he's as Normal as you or I," said Craston.

"I'm inclined to agree with you," said Stramm. "At least, I have observed no powers in him as yet. However, that in no way alters the fact that he may very well be able to bring about Gareth Cole's downfall."

"What's in it for you?" asked Craston.

"I'm afraid I don't quite understand you."

"Come on, Elston," said Craston. "I thought we were going to be frank with each other. Drake is dead, Rysler is a fool, and Povich consists of nothing but fat and tobacco. Gareth Cole has presented no immediate threat to us, and yet you are taking Rysler and Povich along with you to do battle with him. Why? Is it your intention that after the battle is over you and I will be the only two Barons left?"

"It's a possibility," admitted Stramm, "but hardly one upon which I'm planning."

"You are perceptive enough, though, to realize that you and I are the only Barons who are worth a damn?" persisted Craston.

"As long as you seem intent upon putting it that way, yes, of course I realize it. In fact, I've often wondered why you haven't either had me assassinated or asked me to conspire with you."

"Both thoughts have crossed my mind," Craston replied with a smile. "But they were totally unacceptable. I very much doubt that you've ever been in a position where you could be assassinated, or, if so, where your murder could not be traced back to me. As for our forming a conspiracy, I've no doubts that it would work, but since you are the only man alive that I consider my equal in such things, you are by your very competence the one man I do not choose to trust with so ambitious an undertaking. This incidentally, is not to imply that I won't eventually overthrow the Council of Barons. I will, but it will be done in my own good time and on my own terms. Does that surprise you?"

"Not at all," replied Stramm. "Indeed, I would have been surprised had your reasoning not been working in that direction."

"And now, if the word games are over with, why did you really come here? Surely you knew in advance that I wouldn't lend either my name or my army to your little misadventure."

"I came," said Stramm, "to sound you out. I've no doubts that you will refuse to aid us. I'm primarily interested in why you will so refuse."

"Afraid I'll grab all the Baronies while you're out playing with the mutants?" grinned Craston.

"It's a possibility," said Stramm. "So is a deal with Gareth Cole."

"*I'm* going to help the man who blinded me?" laughed Craston. "Come off it, Elston."

"Just a suggestion," replied Stramm. "I'm sure I can come up with others."

"Be my guest. But try to hurry, won't you? I'm much too busy to waste my time in semantics and guesswork."

"All right," said Stramm, suddenly very businesslike. "Let's try this hypothesis on for size. You knew Michael would antagonize Donahoe sooner or later, and you knew that when he did so Donahoe would kill him."

"Go on."

"You further knew that we'd be too heavily committed to the attack on the subways to back off because of Michael's death, especially when he brought it on himself. And, being an intelligent man, you have doubtless reached the same conclusion that I have: namely, that

73

Donahoe is not a mutant—or at least, not possessed of such powers as to present much of a danger to Cole. You would therefore count on the fact that our battle can only result in disaster, thus leaving you unchallenged as the most powerful man in the Hub. And, I might add, commander-in-chief of the bulk of our armies."

"Very good, Elston," said Craston. "Very good indeed."

"Quite simple," said Stramm. "As plain as the nose on your face."

"As long as it isn't as plain as the noses on Aldan's and Gerald's faces," laughed Craston. "As for my own nose, I haven't seen it for a long time."

"Well," said Stramm, rising, "I'll detain you from your business no longer. I just wanted to ascertain whether my thoughts on the matter were correct."

"Just a minute!" snapped Craston, also rising.

"Yes?" inquired Stramm, turning to face him.

Craston strode across the room to the door, his steps sure, his demeanor that of a sighted man. When he reached it he turned back to Stramm, leaning against it. He seemed perfectly relaxed, yet Stramm could see little ripples of muscle tensing in his neck, as if he were prepared to defend his position against the door no matter what the cost.

"You realize, of course," he said at last, "that we're not through yet. In fact, we're only halfway there. You can stand or sit as you choose. Personally, I'd suggest the latter. You might as well make yourself comfortable, since I believe you're going to be my guest for a bit longer."

Stramm sat down in a hard-backed chair. "All right, Andrew. Now what?"

"Now we try to figure out why, since everything you've said thus far is quite true, you still intend to go through with the attack."

Stramm settled back and folded his arms across his

narrow chest. "*You* figure it out, Andrew," he said. *I* already know."

"Obviously you expect to win," said Craston. "Even if you had no sense of self-preservation, you would never let all the Baronies fall into my hands. It is also apparent that a force of six hundred men has absolutely no chance to defeat Cole's mutants and monsters; nor could you, Aldan and Gerald, by virtue either of your courage or sagacity, turn the battle in your favor. Therefore, you must be counting on Donahoe to dispose of Cole."

"Well reasoned," said Stramm, clapping his hands and enjoying the startled expression that crossed Craston's face at the sudden sound. "And now that you know my plans, I think I shall take my leave of you."

"Not just yet, Elston," said Craston. "Any child could have deduced that. I want to know why you believe Donahoe can defeat Cole."

"I'm not at all sure he can," said Stramm.

Craston narrowed his lids over his sightless eyes for a moment, then continued. "I believe you, Elston. Obviously, if Donahoe was certain he could destroy Cole, he would have done it long ago—or else he has no desire to do so, and is in fact in Cole's employ at this very moment."

"A distinct possibility," offered Stramm.

"Then why are you risking your life, very likely throwing it away, to do battle with Cole?"

"Maybe I'm just considering the alternatives," said Stramm. "What if Donahoe defeated Cole without my help? Where would I be then?"

"In much the same position you are now," said Craston. "And that is not an unenviable position. No, you're far too intelligent to risk everything you have without a better reason than that."

"Maybe I'm just being patriotic."

"To what purpose? Your status will not be appreciably enhanced by Cole's death. After all, he never leaves his stronghold. If we didn't attack the subways, we'd probably be left in peace."

"Until Cole thinks his army of mutants is strong enough," said Stramm.

"Hell!" exploded Craston. "He doesn't need them. Didn't you tell me he made an appearance in Donahoe's cell?"

"One of his firebirds did."

"And the cell was under maximum security at the time. No, Elston, I'm afraid you'll have to think up another story."

"Not me, Andrew," said Stramm with a smile. "I know why I'm going. If you want to figure it out, *you* make up the story."

"You'll have to bear with me for a minute or two, and I'll do just that."

"How?"

"By eliminating all the wrong reasons," said Craston. "Deduction by negation has its uses. To begin with, I'm afraid I'm going to have to write off patriotism as a possible reason for your actions; no man of your intelligence and political power can be as blindly patriotic as you'd like the masses to believe. And since, as I mentioned, Cole doesn't need his mutants to penetrate our defenses, I'll cross military expediency off the list. You're not at all sure Donahoe can do what he says, which means that you're not simply getting on the bandwagon of a sure thing. And, since Cole's living or dying will have little effect on you, that eliminates his possible death as a consideration for a gamble of this magnitude."

"Very logical," commented Stramm. "Unfortunately, you seem to have disposed of all possible reasons for my conduct."

"Not quite," replied Craston. "I think the key word I used was gamble. And that is precisely what this is: a gamble. The odds are disproportionately long for a man of your position and resources; hence the rewards must be as great as they are unlikely."

"You do rattle on endlessly," said Stramm with some irritation.

"Bear with me just a little longer, Elston, I'm almost done. Let's put our heads together and try to figure out what possible benefits would make risking your life against the seeming certainty of defeat acceptable to you."

"Go right ahead."

"I shall. Obviously, you must feel that there is a chance however slight, that Donahoe can defeat Cole. Otherwise this is nothing less than a suicide mission, and I cannot believe you are inclined to throw your life away needlessly. Now, should Donahoe win, what good can that possibly do you that it cannot do for the rest of us?"

"You tell me," said Stramm.

"Must I? I consider it painfully obvious. You have doubtless made a deal with Donahoe, or else exert enough influence over him, so that should he defeat Cole, an alliance between the two of you is a foregone conclusion. He will set you up as the ruler of the Hub, while you will let him . . ." Craston paused, scratching his head.

"Yes, Andrew? While I will let him do what?"

"I'm not sure—but I'll figure that part of it out before long."

"No you won't," said Stramm, "for the simple reason that your logic is faulty. I should think it would be apparent that if Donahoe can defeat Cole, he'll have no need of me or anyone else. In fact, we'll have done little more than trade a rational superman for an irrational one."

"True," said Craston thoughtfully. "Then there can be only one other alternative: you intend to kill Donahoe the instant he destroys Cole."

"Of course. You know, Andrew, sometimes I'm amazed at the way you approach the truth by such circuitous means."

"But that's not enough," persisted Craston. "Obviously you'll be more secure with both Cole and Donahoe dead—but so will the rest of us. There will be no personal and individual gain for you."

"You disappoint me, Andrew. You immediately recognize the fact that I wouldn't risk throwing my life away if it would benefit you as much as me, and yet you fail to follow your own train of reasoning."

"Rubbish! You're an open book, Elston. If you succeed in killing both Cole and Donahoe, you doubtless feel that you can convince Povich and Rysler to disenfranchise me, since I alone of the Barons will not support you. Povich is an old man who will die before long, Rysler is a fool, and with Donahoe dead, Alutha will be yours for the asking."

"That's the gist of it," said Stramm calmly.

"It won't work, and you know it."

"I'd like to know why you think it is foredoomed to failure."

"First of all, the odds are thousands to one against your surviving the raid. It is highly unlikely that Donahoe can kill Cole, and if he manages to do so, even more unlikely that you can kill him. Even granting all of that, I can assure you that I am both prepared and quite able to retain my Barony no matter what you try to do, to me."

"Then you've nothing to worry about," said Stramm.

"Except that you've been lying to me."

"I haven't said a damned thing. These are all your conclusions, not mine."

"And they're insufficient. If your sole objective was

power, there are more practical ways of attaining it. Therefore, I must assume my hypothesis was only partially correct."

"Well," said Stramm easily, "better half a loaf than none at all."

"You are puzzling," admitted Craston. "You came here, ostensibly to get me to join you, yet you have not presented a single acceptable argument. In fact, you seem to have done everything in your power to make my resolve not to support you even firmer. Why?"

"I'm afraid you're going to have to figure that out all by yourself. Now, what answer shall I take back to the others? Are you going to help us, or are you going to sit here and do nothing?"

"I'm going to stay here, of course," said Craston. "You'll all be killed, and then your motivations will become strictly academic."

"It's quite possible," agreed Stramm. He walked to the door and gently pushed Craston aside. "But don't count on it."

CHAPTER TEN

Stramm was tired.

He had walked well over one hundred miles during the past two days, and he honestly believed that the only thing keeping him on his feet was his abhorrence at the thought of keeling over before Donahoe did. He brushed the sweat from his forehead and looked ahead of him. The redbeard was showing no signs of tiring yet, though it was apparent that at least half of his six hundred soldiers would happily have collapsed and refused to march any farther if they thought they could get away with it.

They'd be reaching the entrance to the old Holland Tunnel before too much longer, and Stramm was busily turning over plans and alternatives in his mind. He couldn't repress a grin when he recalled his visit to Craston's apartments. The blind Baron was almost too clever for his own good. He had hit upon most of the reasons both for Stramm's willingness to enter Cole's stronghold and for Stramm's equally strong desire for Craston to remain in the Hub. But his mind was too quick, too devious; it dealt in plots and subterfuges—as, to be sure, did Stramm's—but it rejected the obvious, even when the obvious happened to be true.

Stramm stepped over a fallen log, then paused to flick the ants from his boot. It was necessary to keep off the roads, lest Cole be forewarned of their presence too early, but did that blasted Donahoe have to take them through *every* damned obstacle the forests and fields provided? They had come close to losing a pair of Povich's men in a quicksand pool earlier in the day, and Rysler himself could barely see because of the swelling from a bee sting on his eyelid. This was no way to get their armies in the proper mood for an encounter with a supposedly invincible enemy.

He pushed forward through another patch of thorn bushes, cursing as the little needles tore at his flesh, and, in an effort to get his mind off his immediate physical discomfort, he forced his thoughts back to his conversation with Craston.

The blind Baron had been right in his main assumption: the odds against success were astronomical. Where Craston had been mistaken was in his assumption that there would be one single benefit to be derived from a successful battle that would make the risk seem palatable.

He was wrong, of course. Cole had never once left Manhattan to attack the Hub or any other Normal city, and it would be foolhardy to sacrifice a position of enormous wealth and power simply on the assumption that he might someday change his policy and lead his mutant armies into the field against the Barons.

No, it was a combination of things that had convinced Stramm to enter the subways. No one factor could have outweighed the likelihood of defeat, but when added together there was enough of an advantage to be gained to make the odds seem fair. Not low, but fair.

First, it was entirely possible that Donahoe really had stumbled upon Cole's Achilles' heel. It wasn't too likely, he admitted grimly, but the possibility couldn't be discounted. If that were so, then victory was all but assured with the smallest possible amount of bloodshed. And if a victory over Gareth Cole was accomplished, then there would be an immediate change in the political structure of the Hub. Stramm was the most popular and influential Baron, of that there was no doubt. A few public comments concerning the character of the one Baron who lacked the courage to join in Cole's destruction and, no matter how well prepared Craston

81

was for a physical attack, he would find himself totally unable to withstand an attack on a moral level. He would still control his army, but his influence would end there and it was doubtful that he would be willing to take on the combined military might of the remaining Barons.

With Drake dead and Craston all but powerless, the other two would pose no great problem to him. Povich would be content to live out the short span of time remaining to him in peace and semiseclusion, tending to his gardens, while Rysler was the most easily manipulated Baron of them all. Thus Stramm would have effected a bloodless and almost undetectable coup without ever seeming to aspire to greater power than he now possessed.

Then, too, there was the matter of the military security of the Hub. He agreed with Craston that Donahoe would scarcely be more disposed to amicable relations than Cole had, and would in fact be more likely to conduct an invasion. However, whatever powers Donahoe might have—and Stramm was not yet convinced that he possessed any at all—they were hardly equal to Cole's. And without Cole as an ultimate ace in the hole, the mutant army wouldn't cause them much more trouble than a Normal army.

On this he and Craston agreed. They also agreed that, at present, Cole seemed considerably less hostile than Donahoe. But Craston hadn't reasoned far enough ahead, and therein lay the great desirability of replacing Cole with the redbeard. Cole, for reasons known only to himself—or only to himself and his mutant companions —was obviously conducting breeding experiments which required the periodic capture of Normal women. While Stramm couldn't even guess at the purpose of these experiments, he knew that their success could only be detrimental to the Normals. He further knew that Donahoe didn't have the intellect to breed two dogs, let alone a race of supermen. Hence, it seemed likely to Stramm that the ultimate future of his race depended on eliminating Gareth Cole before his experiments had reached fruition. Craston should have known that too—but that, reflected Stramm, was Craston's problem, not his own.

In fact, Craston's failure to reason that out was the prime reason he had had to make the blind Baron stay behind. If the battle were not totally one-sided, he could easily foresee an attempt by the blind Baron to assassinate himself, Rysler and Povich and then retreat back to the Hub, never to make war against Cole again, and it was Stramm's solid conviction that the future of Normal society depended on the continued harassment and ultimate defeat of Cole. A secondary consideration was that Craston's absence assured Stramm of a political takeover in the event of a successful battle.

He did not for an instant overlook the overwhelming possibility of defeat. If defeated, neither he nor his men could hope for any mercy from Cole. No one but Donahoe knew him, and it didn't seem too likely that Cole would grant amnesty either to the redbeard or his supporters. And if this was really just an enormous trap cooked up by Cole and Donahoe, then the whole purpose of it was to kill as many Normals as possible—and the Barons would doubtless be the first to die.

He broke out of the brush and found himself on the near-barren field that led to the Holland Tunnel's entrance. The midday sun once again beat down upon him, half-blinding him and almost convincing him that hell would almost be a pleasure after this. He trudged across the field, forcing his feet forward one step at a time, shivering as an occasional drop of sweat raced down the length of his spine.

A few minutes later Donahoe came to a stop and

waited for the straggling armies to catch up with him.

"We're here," announced the redbeard needlessly. "Let's move in."

"No," said Stramm firmly. "We'll wait until nightfall."

"What in Rath for?" demanded Donahoe. "You'll just be giving Gareth more time to prepare his defenses."

"He won't need any if our men don't get a chance to rest," replied Stramm. "We'll let them sit around here for a few hours until the sun goes down. It'll be cooler then, and they'll be a little fresher. The subways have no sunlight anyway, so the time of day won't make any difference. As for Cole, if he isn't already prepared for us, then I hardly think we have anything to worry about. I imagine he can mobilize his mutants and produce his monsters in a matter of minutes, if not seconds—and don't forget: we've got to tear down our barricade before we can get to him."

"That's right," muttered the redbeard. "I forgot all about the damned wall."

"I have a suggestion," said Rysler. "As long as the barricade *does* exist, why don't we rest beside it? I think it would keep the men cooler, and it just might alleviate a little of their uneasiness about being inside the tunnels."

Rysler's idea was adopted, and a few moments later they were walking down the damp main corridor of the Holland Tunnel. An odor of moisture and rot assailed Stramm's nostrils, but he was happy to be free of the burning intensity of the sun, and so he continued his rapid pace. A few rats scurried away before the columns of soldiers, and Stramm estimated that there were well over one thousand hidden rodents for each one he could see. It was not a comforting thought.

He had a number of other disquieting thoughts, foremost of which was the knowledge that they would probably all be dead in a matter of hours. Suddenly his plans and value judgments seemed very foolish to him. Craston was the one man he didn't want to gain total power, and yet the odds were all in favor of Craston's being the sole living Baron by the next·evening.

He had no intention of giving up now, of turning back and allowing Cole to operate unhindered, but it did seem like a good time to hedge his bets. The invasion had been his idea, and for personal as well as altruistic reasons he had to go through with it. It was also obvious that Donahoe was the only irreplaceable member of the war party; no other single man would be missed.

He toyed with the thought for awhile. Then, his decision made, he walked over to Rysler.

"Gerald," he began, "I think we'd better split up our forces to make sure that someone survives this tussle."

"Agreed," said Rysler. "But what will *he* say?"

"You mean Donahoe? I doubt that he'll give much of a damn. He's too intent on killing Cole to worry about how many men are behind him."

"How shall we go about it?"

"In a manner I think may surprise you," said Stramm, with just a trace of an ironic grin.

CHAPTER ELEVEN

—*They're coming, Gareth.*
  —*Yes, Jon. I know.*
  —*Shouldn't we do something about them?*
  —*I've already attended to it, Jon.*

CHAPTER TWELVE

Elston Stramm pushed a loose stone back into place, and leaned against the reconstructed barricade, breathing heavily.

"I don't like it," said Povich. "You've cut off our only line of retreat."

"Had to be done," said Stramm. "If we should lose, which is quite possible, we don't want to let the enemy simply walk through the Holland Tunnel and sneak up on our people without any warning."

"Yes," said Povich impatiently, "but to leave Gerald and all of his men back there—that may well have been the deciding factor. I have the strangest premonition that we may have thrown the battle away even before it's begun."

"I doubt it," said Stramm. "If the mutant really knows Cole's weakness, four hundred men should be able to carry the day. If not, I doubt that four thousand would do us much good."

"I don't know," said Povich. "I think it's entirely possible that the mutant is leading us into a trap."

"Frankly," replied Stramm, "I suspect that he is."

"*What!*" demanded Povich. "And yet you let us—and four hundred other men—be led into it, and even go so far as to see to it that we can't possibly escape?"

"Yes," said Stramm. "Actually, the barricade was replaced strictly for psychological reasons. I have no doubts that Cole can destroy it in two seconds if he's so inclined. I had Rysler replace it solely to convince our men that there can be no turning back."

"But what if we should have to turn back?" demanded Povich.

"If we should have to turn back, then we are dead men anyway," said Stramm. "This will give them a courage born of necessity."

"Why are we here at all if this is a trap?" said Povich, looking worried. "You obviously have a reason—what is it?"

"Look at it logically, Aldan," answered Stramm. "If Cole could kill us all while we were in the Hub, I cannot conceive of any reason why he should not have done so. Therefore, it would appear that he is luring us here because there are certain limitations to his powers, even though we don't know what these limitations are. And I, for one, am perfectly willing to be lured here. After all, we've been trying to get into the subways ever since he began breeding mutants."

"You still haven't answered my question," said Povich doggedly. "Why are you walking into a trap?"

"Because if it *is* a trap, that means Donahoe is still vital to Cole, either as a general or in some other capacity. And the moment Donahoe gives me the slightest indication that he is in Cole's employ, I intend to kill him on the spot. I'll be right behind him, and I suspect he'll be dead before he quite knows what hit him."

"How will that help the rest of us?" demanded Povich, puffing furiously away at his pipe.

"Hopefully, it may throw Cole's—or Donahoe's—army into temporary disarray, possibly enough so we can get through to Cole himself. Even if it doesn't, it will rob Cole of his second in command."

"And even if that happens, we may all still die."

"I admit the possibility," replied Stramm, "but should that come to pass, Rysler will return to the Hub with the certain knowledge that no Normal can ever again attempt to penetrate the subways while Cole lives."

"In other words," said Povich hotly, "you've made us all guinea pigs to see what Cole and Donahoe will or won't be able to do."

"It's a small price to pay," Stramm shrugged, "if it will insure the future of the race."

"But why you and I?" persisted Povich. "Why not just send our men and let the two of us stay behind with Rysler?"

"Because we both know our men wouldn't follow Donahoe into the subways if we remained behind. One of us may fall early in the battle, so I felt a minimum of two Barons would be necessary to avoid complete demoralization if and when one of us falls. Three or four would have been even better, but Michael is dead, Andrew refused to come, and one Baron had to return home if we were defeated. Hence, I could only choose two of us. Since it is my own plan, I felt it fair that I be one, and I quite coldbloodedly chose you because you are considerably older than Gerald." He paused, then smiled and spoke again. "Cheer up. If I'm wrong about it being a trap, there's still a chance we may accomplish what we set out to do. Donahoe may really know of some method of defeating Cole, and though I'm prepared for the contrary, I feel we should proceed as if he were on our side."

"Speaking of Donahoe," said Povich, his lisp lessening as his temper subsided somewhat, "where has he gone to?"

"Up ahead somewhere," said Stramm. "After all, he's the only one who knows his way around the subway system."

"I didn't know this was part of it."

"It's not," replied Stramm, "but as I understand it, the entrance to the surface had been sealed off for centuries. They've built a couple of connecting tunnels to the subways, and that seems to be the only way out of here."

"I suppose we'd best stop talking and catch up with the others," said Povich, thoughtfully taking a puff from his pipe. They headed off in the direction the redbeard had gone. Before long the sound of footsteps echoed down the tunnel, and, following them, they had soon rejoined their forces.

Donahoe was in the lead, walking confidently through the darkened corridor. When he saw the two Barons, he paused until they caught up with him.

"I think, now that I've sealed us in here," began Stramm, "that you might give us some inkling as to how you plan to conduct this little war."

"We're marching straight to Gareth's rooms, and we'll kill anything that stands in our way," was the redbeard's answer.

"I don't suppose you'd like to tell us *how*," said Stramm sardonically.

"Listen," said Donahoe intensely. "Those damned firebirds can be hurt. I know—I've done it. I don't know how and I don't know why, but I do know I damned near killed one of them the day before I set out for the Hub. I say just hack away at them and let's see what happens."

"That's none too comforting an answer," said Povich dubiously.

"Perhaps it is," said Stramm thoughtfully. "After all, Aldan, *we've* never been able to harm one." He turned to Donahoe. "What about Cole's army?"

The redbeard snorted contemptuously. "If that was all we had to worry about, I'd take care of them without your help. Zameth! I could fight the lot of them barehanded and come out of it without a scratch!"

With that he began walking again, coming at last to a small tunnel along the left-hand wall. He turned into it, with Stramm and Povich close on his heels.

"Where are we now?" demanded Povich.

"Heading for the main tunnels," replied Donahoe. "They're about a mile away."

"Why doesn't Cole try to stop us?" said the old Baron. "Can it be that he is unaware of our presence?"

90

"He's aware of it, all right," said the redbeard grimly. "He'll fight us when he's good and ready."

"I don't like the looks of this," said Stramm softly.

"Scared, Norman?" taunted the redbeard.

"Puzzled," came the reply.

"What about?" asked Povich.

"Something's wrong," said Stramm. "Surely Cole knows we're here. He must also know how we plan to fight him, and any alternative plans we might have devised. It seems to me that if we posed even a slight threat to him he would have been ready for us the instant we broke through the barricade. He wouldn't be letting us come this close to him if he thought there was a chance he might lose."

"Bah!" snorted the redbeard. "He'll lose, all right. Now, are you coming or going back to hide with Rysler?"

"We're committed to it," said Stramm grimly. "That doesn't mean we have to like the way it's progressing."

They had been walking while conversing, and they now emerged into a somewhat wider tunnel, which was lit solely by blue-green lights. Stramm glanced apprehensively around, giving special attention to the darkened cubicles that lined the way.

Suddenly a man appeared directly in front of them, where none had been before. He stared solemnly at Stramm and Povich for perhaps twenty seconds, then vanished.

"What the hell was that?" demanded Stramm. Half a hundred of his men were asking the same question.

"It was Raal," said Donahoe.

"Who, or what, is Raal?" asked Stramm.

"One of Gareth's freaks," shrugged the redbeard. "He does things like that."

"I think we'd better get out of here," said Povich, not noticing that his pipe had gone out.

"He just did it to scare you," said Donahoe.

"From the looks of the men, I'd say he did a pretty good job of it," opined Stramm.

"They're Normans," said Donahoe, as if that explained everything. Without another word he began advancing again. After a moment's hesitation Povich followed him. So did the warriors, obviously reluctant but still disciplined.

"How much farther?" whispered Stramm after they had covered another two hundred yards.

"Soon," said the redbeard in his natural voice. He had long since realized that whispering, or even thinking, could safeguard neither his presence nor his intentions.

Stramm turned to his men. "Draw your weapons!" he ordered. "We're closing in on Cole's headquarters. If he's going to do anything, he'll have to do it soon, so be—"

He was cut off in midsentence by a hideous roar. Turning, he saw Donahoe locked in fierce hand-to-hand combat with a monster straight out of a terrified child's nightmare. Covered with scales, breathing smoke and flame, shaped in a grotesque caricature of a man, it had locked its enormous arms around the redbeard. while Donahoe landed blow after blow upon its head.

Stramm barely had time to take in the situation before it was altered by the presence of a dozen more such beasts. He drew his sword and charged into their midst. His army responded to the challenge, and soon the ancient subway tunnel was transformed into a bloody battleground. The floor was awash with gore as more and more of the monsters appeared and more and more of his men sank to the ground, never to rise again.

Then, from the corner of his eye, he saw Donahoe triumphantly waving the severed head of the first beast. Stramm's eyes lit up and he redoubled his efforts. *They could be killed!* Donahoe had been right after all!

A huge talon raked Stramm's back and he fell to

one knee, losing his sword in the process. Fumbling around blindly, he finally found the hilt of another one and rose just in time to bear the brunt of a new creature's charge. Sidestepping carefully, he drove the point of his weapon into the creature's eye. It emitted a howl of pain and turned back upon him. He was ready for it and, ducking under the outstretched arms, he buried his weapon into the nightmare thing's belly. It roared and collapsed, coughing up gobs of a slimy green substance.

The battle raged back and forth along the length of the tunnel for the better part of an hour. Finally, the last of the monsters lay dead upon the floor.

Panting heavily, drenched in sweat and blood, Donahoe and Stramm surveyed the carnage. Perhaps fifty men still lived; Povich was not among them.

"We've won!" screamed the redbeard triumphantly.

Stramm forced a smile for Donahoe's sake, but his eyes kept darting around. *It can't be this easy,* he thought. *Not after nine centuries of defeat.*

He was right.

There was a sudden silence, so strong as to be almost tangible. Then he saw it.

It was like nothing he had ever seen before, nothing he was even capable of imagining. It half-slithered, half-rolled across the floor, sucking up men into its folds of protoplasm, a gigantic vacuum cleaner of fetid flesh.

Now only fifteen men remained, now only ten, and then Stramm charged at it, hacking and hewing as he went. Then he, too, was engulfed.

Donahoe stood alone, sword drawn, glaring at the pulsating mass.

"Come on, Gareth!" he screamed. "Send it after me! This is no puny Norman it's facing! This is Red Will Donahoe, and I'm not leaving here until I've got your head hanging from my belt!"

The thing vanished, and then he appeared, small,

pale, slender, looking like anything but the most powerful being in the world.

"That was a stupid thing to do, barbarian," Cole said calmly. "You cost four hundred innocent men their lives."

"*I* didn't kill them!" snapped the redbeard.

"For all practical purposes you did," replied Cole. "You must have known I would defend myself."

"I'll kill you yet!" promised the redbeard.

"I think not," said Cole. "However, I won't stop you from trying."

"Huh?" The redbeard stared at him dumbly.

"You're free to go, barbarian."

"Why?" He narrowed his eyes, sure it was a trick, trying to see through it.

"You haven't yet outlived your usefulness to me," replied Cole. "You can traverse the tunnels at will and no one will harm you. However, anyone accompanying you will be destroyed. Is that clear, barbarian?"

"As clear as *this!*" roared Donahoe, hurling his war-club at the fragile body. Cole allowed himself the luxury of a smile as the club turned to dust long before it reached its mark.

CHAPTER THIRTEEN

"Dead? All of them?" demanded Craston, his blind eyes staring blankly across the room at Rysler. "How did it happen?"

"I don't know," answered Rysler, shifting his weight uneasily from one foot to the other. He was always uncomfortable in Craston's drab, dark living quarters; today, as he broke the news of the defeat to the sightless Baron, he was doubly so.

"Why didn't you help them?"

"When we heard the fighting we tried to tear down the barricade," said Rysler, "but we couldn't budge so much as a pebble of it. I'm sure Cole had something to do with it."

"Then how do you know they're dead?"

"About an hour later the barricade went back to normal. We began disassembling it and met Donahoe, who had been working on it from the other side. He told us what had happened."

"And you believed him?"

"We believed that he was the sole survivor, yes. But it's pretty hard to believe that the whole thing wasn't a setup, and we took him prisoner."

"Where is he now?" asked Craston.

"He escaped."

"How?"

"He managed to work his bonds free during the night, and by daybreak he was nowhere to be seen. I've got fifty men out hunting for him right now."

"You needn't have bothered," said Craston decisively. "He's on his way here right now."

"He is?" exclaimed Rysler. "How do you know?"

"Where else could he go?" replied Craston, making no attempt to hide his contempt for Rysler's reasoning processes.

"Where else?" repeated Rysler. "Back to the subways, of course!"

"Gerald, you're even more stupid than I had thought."

"What do you mean?" asked Rysler hotly.

"You still don't realize that Donahoe was telling the truth all along—that he truly intended to kill Gareth Cole, and that he was trapped along with the rest of Stramm's and Povich's men."

"You're crazy! If that were true, then why was he the only one to survive? Why didn't Cole kill him too?"

"I've no idea," said Craston. "But I do know that Donahoe was on our side."

"Prove it," insisted Rysler.

"Certainly. If it was a trap, why did he permit you and your men to remain beyond the barricade? Why did he return to you after Stramm and Povich were defeated? And if he was really in Gareth Cole's employ, why did he once again place himself in your power after Povich and Stramm were killed?"

"I don't know," said Rysler slowly. "But I also don't know why Cole let him live if they're deadly enemies."

"Maybe it's impossible for Cole to have a deadly enemy," suggested the blind Baron. "Maybe no man alive poses a threat to Cole."

"Then why did he kill our men and let Donahoe live?" demanded Rysler.

"I don't know," said Craston, "but I'm willing to make an educated guess. I think Cole killed our men because he had no use for them, and he let Donahoe live because he needs him."

"As what?"

"As a general, I suppose," said Craston, vaguely feeling that he only had half the answer. "But whatever the reason, I am convinced that Donahoe will not be returning to the subways—and if he doesn't go back to Cole, then in all likelihood he is on his way here."

"Even though he knows we're out to get him?" said Rysler skeptically.

"Take my word for it."

"Not without a reason," said Rysler. "In fact, I'll be sending the rest of my men out into the countryside in search of him within the next few hours, after they've rested and gotten some food in their stomachs."

"As you will," said Craston, with just a trace of a smile about his lips.

Rysler stalked to the door.

"And Gerald," Craston called after him, "if I were you, I should see to it that Donahoe is killed on sight."

After his ears told him Rysler had left, he turned his sightless eyes to another door at the far end of the chamber.

"You may come in now, Joshua."

A tall, balding man dressed in military apparel entered the room.

"You were listening, I presume?" asked Craston.

"I was."

"Well, what do you make of it?"

"I agree with you that Donahoe tried to lead a successful attack against the subways," said the man called Joshua, "but I fail to see why you feel he'll be coming here for refuge."

"Not for refuge, Joshua," said Craston. "Not for refuge."

"I see," said Joshua. "All steps will be taken to protect your person. I'll double the guard and . . ."

"Idiot!" exploded Craston. "You're as dense as Rysler! Can only a blind man see what's happening?"

"I'm afraid I don't understand, sir."

"He doesn't want *me!*" yelled Craston. "And he doesn't want Gerald either!"

"Then what—"

"Think, man! Think!" shrilled Craston. "Where is the

97

one place in the Hub that Donahoe will feel he migh be able to go with some degree of safety?"

"I don't know, sir," said Joshua stiffly.

"To Michael Drake's castle! Don't you understand? I he can convince enough people that he didn't purposely lead us into a trap, then he has a legal claim to Drake's Barony."

Joshua's eyes narrowed. "And that means—"

"Exactly!" said Craston. "With Povich dead, the man who marries Alutha Drake will inherit that Barony as well. And that makes Donahoe potentially the most powerful man in the Hub."

"But is he bright enough to realize that, sir?"

"Of course not!" snapped Craston. "But Alutha will figure it out. She might even form a political alliance with him."

"I doubt it," said Joshua.

"A week ago you'd have doubted that only two Barons would be alive today," replied Craston.

"Then you want me to take our men to Drake's castle?" asked Joshua, knowing the answer.

"The sooner the better," replied Craston. "And if you get there in time, you might put Alutha Drake out of her widow's misery, just to be on the safe side."

"It will be done," promised Joshua. "One question, sir. I don't like the thought of leaving you unprotected. If Donahoe doesn't show up soon, how long do you want us to wait?"

"You needn't worry about that," said Craston, staring sightlessly at his underling. "He'll show up, all right."

And he did.

CHAPTER FOURTEEN

It upset him, having to skulk through the shadows of Michael Drake's castle like a thief. He would much rather have burst in through the main entrance hall, proclaiming to all within earshot that he was Red Will Donahoe, come to claim what was his. But those blasted Normans hadn't believed his story when he returned from Gareth Cole's bloodbath, and he was sure word had gotten back to the Hub that he was once again to be considered a deadly enemy with a price on his head—especially if his head was no longer attached to his body.

So, for once, discretion had overcome valor, and after sneaking in through a side entrance he was proceeding down a long, narrow corridor, seeking the spoils of his conquest. Belatedly it occurred to him that Drake's wife was in all probability quartered on the second or third floor, further removed from any and all threats of violence, and he ascended to the next level of the castle as soon as he came across a stairwell.

At the top of the stairs he saw a light emanating from an open room about halfway down another hallway. Silent and ominous as some giant jungle cat he approached it, flattening himself against the wall and carefully peering around the corner of the doorway.

Alutha Drake sat on a plain wooden chair, staring out a window at the fields below. Before she had any intimation that she was no longer alone, the redbeard had clasped a massive hand across her mouth and, drawing her head back, he placed a dagger against her unprotected throat.

"One sound and you're a dead woman!" he whispered fiercely.

Her body tensed, then relaxed, and he released his grip.

"You know who I am?"

She nodded mutely, her eyes darting to the doorway through which he had entered.

"Then you know what I've come for."

"No," she said.

"I've come for Alutha Drake. Where is she?"

"I am the wife of the man you killed."

"He had it coming," growled the redbeard. He stepped back and ran his eyes over her body from head to foot. "I can't say too much for his taste in women," he said at last.

"Nor I for his taste in murderers," she snapped, surprised at her boldness.

"Murder?" repeated the redbeard. "Murder be damned! He was armed, and I killed him with my bare hands! Red Will Donahoe doesn't have to murder anyone—and especially not a Norman."

"The word is Normal," she replied coldly, "although I'm sure you can't begin to comprehend the concept."

"You'll have plenty of time to teach me, now that you belong to me," he said.

"I belong to no one!"

"We'll argue about that in the morning," he grinned, reaching out for her arm.

"You'll never live to see the sun rise," she said in level tones.

"I suppose you're going to make sure of it," he snorted.

"What makes you think that your whereabouts are known only to me?" she countered.

"No one saw me come in," he said confidently.

"No one had to. They'll know you're here and they'll come after you."

"Hah! Nobody'll know unless Gareth tells them, and Gareth won't tell a Norman anything."

"Craston will know. He'll figure it out. In fact, I wouldn't be at all surprised to learn that his men are already on their way here."

"Craston? That blind idiot?" Donahoe roared with laughter.

"He'll know," she said with certainty, "and he'll send his men. Use my body if you like, murderer, but every second you spend here will put Craston's men one second closer to avenging my husband's death."

Something in her attitude made him pause. She seemed so sure, so absolutely convinced of the truth of her guesswork. Donahoe ran a hand through his long, shaggy red hair. Could she be right? Could Craston or Rysler somehow figure out that he had returned to the Hub? And even if they could, would they be able to guess that he had come to Drake's castle? He shook his head vigorously. No! It would be too much of a coincidence . . . and yet, she seemed so certain, even to the point of offering him her body to detain him.

The problem was too great for him. He shrugged and made a decision along easier lines. He had started the evening like a scared rabbit; he would end it like one.

Grabbing Alutha by the arm, he walked out the door and over to the stairwell. Her body would afford him just as much comfort in the plains beyond the city as in her bedroom, and then, if by some fluke of chance she happened to have guessed right, he'd still be alive to enjoy her again the next morning.

They had descended the stairs and were heading toward the small door through which he had gained entry to the castle when he heard a jumble of sounds coming from the other side of it. Swiftly he drew back into a corner.

"Who are they?" he hissed.

"Craston's men."

"How can you tell?"

"Who else could it be?" she said coldly. "You've managed to kill all the others."

"You were right," he mumbled, taking a quick peek as Joshua walked into the castle, followed by a number of armed men. "But how did they know I'd come here?" he whispered, genuinely puzzled. Alutha stared at him contemptuously.

Then he heard Joshua's voice, speaking in low muffled tones. "Any sign of Donahoe?"

"No," came a faint reply.

"Then we're ahead of him. Where is the widow?"

"Upstairs, I suspect."

"Good. Don't forget: it must look like Donahoe came here and killed her. Make it good and bloody."

"What about Drake's servants?" said another voice.

"How many of them are there?" asked Joshua.

"About ten."

"I suppose we'll have to kill them too," said Joshua. He began climbing up the stairs, followed by his warriors.

Donahoe had been watching Alutha's face. At first it registered shock, then gradually changed to a look of shrewd understanding. "When they find out I'm not upstairs," she whispered, "they'll search the entire castle."

"Why do they want to kill you?" asked Donahoe.

"Promise not to touch me and I'll tell you," she said.

"I don't make deals with Normans!" he snapped.

"You'll make a deal with this one or I'm going to scream for help."

"No you won't," he said confidently. "If they find you they'll kill you."

"And if you don't make that promise, you'll wind up killing me too. At least this way I won't die alone, or in vain."

"You mean it, don't you?" said Donahoe, looking deep into her cold, clear eyes. "You'll really call them."

"I will."

"All right," he growled. "It's a deal. Come on!"

He took a firm grip on her wrist and walked boldly to the door. Once outside he began to head in the southerly direction from which he had come.

"Not that way," whispered Alutha.

"Why not?"

"Joshua will have left a few men around the grounds."

"What makes you think they'll be here? The tunnels are the other way."

"Rysler's men weren't here. That means he's probably patrolling the area between the Hub and the roads leading to the subways."

"That doesn't make sense," protested Donahoe. "He knows I didn't come here by any roads; why should he think I'll be returning on them—or that I'll be returning at all."

"I don't know," she admitted. "I just think you—we—would be safer going off to the west."

"So I can walk right into the hands of Drake's army?" asked the redbeard sardonically. "Is that where you're hiding them? To the west?"

"There is no army," she said. "It dispersed after you murdered my husband."

Tired of arguing, Donahoe grunted and began walking again. Before he was halfway across the broad fields surrounding the castle he found himself face to face with two of Joshua's sentries.

Before the shock of recognition had left their faces he had hurled his warclub into the face of one and pounced upon the other, dragging him to the ground. The man fought back fiercely, pummeling Donahoe's head with his fists, but he was no match for the redbeard. Shrugging off the effects of the blows, Donahoe drew his dagger and plunged it into the side of the man's neck. A stream of blood spurted out, momentarily blinding him, but when he recovered his vision he discovered that the knife had done its job. The man lay face down on the ground, strange gurgling noises rasping forth from his throat. In another minute he shuddered convulsively and lay still.

The redbeard jumped to his feet, looking wildly around, half-expecting Alutha to have vanished into the darkness. But she stood where he had released her, half a dozen paces away from the corpse of his first victim. He retrieved his warclub, shoved it through his belt, and turned to her again.

"You were right," he said, puzzled.

"Yes."

"There will be more, won't there?"

"Probably," she said, "and next time you may not be lucky enough to kill them before they get off a scream or two."

"Which way should we go?"

"West."

He nodded his acquiescence and headed off in that direction. Then, as if he had forgotten something, he turned and reached out to grab Alutha's wrist.

"Don't worry. I'll follow you," she said, backing away.

"See that you do."

"I will. And don't forget your promise."

"My promise?"

"Never to touch me again. Not even my wrist."

"I'll keep it, all right," he growled. "You're more trouble than you're worth. Don't know how in Rath Drake ever forced himself to touch you."

He looked up. A cloud was obscuring the moon, and if they hurried they could reach the cover of the forest beyond the fields before Joshua and his warriors discovered that the castle was empty.

CHAPTER FIFTEEN

By morning they had put a good fifteen miles between themselves and Drake's castle. Donahoe had frequently departed from his westerly direction in the hopes of throwing his pursuers off the track, and had crossed and recrossed a number of small streams to further confuse them.

Now, as they came to a secluded glade at the edge of a densely overgrown forest, he sat down, propping his back against the bole of a tree, and gestured to Alutha to do the same.

"Yes, I suppose we're safe here for a few minutes," she said, seating herself about five yards away from him.

"Where are we?" he asked gruffly, picking up a small branch and breaking off minute pieces of it.

"I'm not sure," replied Alutha. "As far as I can remember, there are no villages or cities ahead of us."

"Then why in Rath did you tell me to come this way?" the redbeard exploded.

"To make it harder for Craston's men to find us," she replied. "And also because we have no place better to go."

"What do you mean?"

"It should be apparent even to you," she replied irritably, brushing a strand of hair back off her forehead, "that neither of us can return to any Normal city without being killed."

"Which reminds me—why did Craston want to kill you?"

"Because I am Michael Drake's widow and Aldan Povich's daughter."

"So what?" asked the redbeard.

"I represent a political threat to his power."

"Why? I thought only men could become Barons."

"True. But I am my father's sole surviving heir."

"What's that supposed to mean?" asked Donahoe, trying to leap ahead to what she obviously felt was a logical conclusion but not quite being able to do so.

"It means that the man who marries me will inherit not only my husband's Barony but my father's as well. And Elston Stramm left no survivors."

"Then that means that whoever marries you would be twice as powerful as Craston or Rysler!" said Donahoe, finally seeing the light. "And with the power he held, he'd probably be able to take over Stramm's holdings as well."

"That's correct."

"And since I own you . . ."

"You do *not* own me!"

"And since I own you," he continued, ignoring her, "that would make me the greatest man in the Hub!"

"Nothing would make you the greatest man in the Hub, or anywhere else," she said coldly. "But it *would* make you the most politically powerful one."

"What's the difference?" he laughed, picking up another fallen branch and snapping it in two.

"I wouldn't expect one of Gareth Cole's lackeys to know," she said, turning away and looking off into the woods.

"I'm no lackey of Cole's!" he exploded fiercely. "Before I'm done I'll have that freak's head as a trophy!"

"There's nobody here but me, murderer," she said, turning back to him. "You don't have to pretend."

"Pretend? What in Rath are you talking about?"

"Are you actually trying to tell me that you didn't know you were leading Elston and my father into a trap?" she demanded unbelievingly.

"It was no trap! And we damned near beat him!"

"Except that you lost four hundred men and he lost no one," she said cynically.

"Next time," he promised. "Next time I'll get him."

"With four hundred more men?" she scoffed.

"By myself."

"Sure."

"By Zameth, I mean it!" he roared. "I'll tear that damned blond midget's head off his body!"

"You're quite an actor," she said. "When you say it like that I almost believe you."

"You'd better!" he growled, staring sullenly at the ground while forming mental pictures of Gareth Cole's death throes.

"Why do you hate him so?"

"How would *you* like to live in a sunless hole in the ground with a bunch of freaks who know everything you're thinking, and can tell you what you're going to do even before you know it yourself?"

"But you're one of them."

"I'm not one of Gareth's freaks!" he bellowed.

"Then why do you live with them?" she persisted.

"I was born there."

"What are your powers?"

"I haven't got any."

"Then what qualifies you to be Cole's general?"

"I'm the best man he's got," he replied with characteristic immodesty.

"That can't be enough," she said. "Surely a telepath could do as well or better."

"Zameth!" he roared. "You sound like Stramm! I don't know why Gareth does what he does! Why don't you ask him?"

She stared at him for a long moment, then shrugged and got to her feet. "I think we'd better be going," she said. "They're doubtless still on our trail."

He nodded, arose, and began walking again. Noon found them another ten miles removed from the castle, and by evening they had almost doubled the distance, thanks to a long stretch of flat, barren ground and the remnants of an ancient highway.

As darkness fell he noticed her feet beginning to drag and once again came to a halt.

"We'll spend the night here," he said gruffly. "When's the last time you ate?"

"Yesterday noon," she said hoarsely, brushing the dust and sweat from her face.

"It's too dark to hunt down any animals," he said. "We'll have to make do with roots and berries. There are enough of them growing around here."

"They'll do," she said, leaning against a tree and suddenly realizing how thoroughly exhausted she was. "I'm terribly tired. Would you please gather some for me?"

"I don't own you, remember?"

"I don't understand what you mean," she said, puzzled.

"Get 'em yourself," said the redbeard, going off to fill his stomach.

CHAPTER SIXTEEN

"And you found no trace of them at all?" asked Craston, sitting on a soft chair in his small dining chamber.

"No, sir," said Joshua. "We trailed them for the better part of a week, but he's a cagey devil. He'd go into a stream, walk through the water for a mile or more, come out on the same side he entered, then cross it twenty yards further on. I've still got some men on the trail, but he's got to be making far better time. I'm afraid it's a lost cause."

"No cause is ever lost," said the blind Baron. "Is Alutha Drake still with him?"

"Yes, sir."

"The fact that he hasn't killed or abandoned her would seem to imply that he is aware of her worth to him, would it not?" said Craston slowly.

"Yes, sir," Joshua replied mechanically.

"And the only way he can cash in on her is to return to the Hub to lay claim to the Baronies," continued Craston. "Therefore, we needn't worry too much about catching up with him. It would be nice to do away with him far away from here, to be sure, but the fact remains that he'll be returning eventually. All we have to do is wait for him."

"For how long?"

"Not very," said Craston with certainty. "He is neither a patient nor a subtle man. And of course, if Alutha either dies or escapes from him he's lost whatever advantage he might have had. Hence, he'll doubtless be returning before either of those events comes to pass."

"Unless Cole kills him in the meantime," offered Joshua.

"Nonsense. Cole won't kill him. If he'd wanted to, he could have done it when he killed Elston and Aldan. No, Donahoe will be back, mark my words." He allowed himself the luxury of a chuckle. "And if I know Alutha Drake, he won't be able to get back soon enough."

CHAPTER SEVENTEEN

"What's he like?"

"What's who like?"

"Gareth Cole."

"Again?" winced the redbeard. "I've been telling you for ten days now."

"But you haven't told me what I want to know," said Alutha.

"His weakness?" grimaced Donahoe. "He hasn't got any."

"He *must* have one, and a big one," insisted Alutha, stepping around a tree which had fallen during a recent thunderstorm. "If he didn't have one, he'd rule the world."

"He rules as much of it as he's interested in," said Donahoe, withdrawing his knife and hacking away at some undergrowth which blocked his path. "Believe me, if Gareth wanted to be king of the world, he would be."

"And yet you think you're going to kill him," she said, almost smiling.

"I know it," he said devoutly.

"I still don't know why you hate him so. After all, from what you've told me I'd say that he alone was responsible for keeping you alive."

"He should have killed me when he had the chance!" spat the redbeard.

She shook her head. "I can't understand why anyone would wish to die."

"Of course you can't," he growled, wielding his knife with renewed vigor. "Nobody who hasn't lived in the tunnels could imagine what it's like."

"I guess you're right."

111

"To walk through a crowded, absolutely silent tunnel and then hear everyone suddenly break out in laughter because someone told a joke that only you couldn't hear," he said, more to himself than to her. "To read a book word by word, page by page, when all Gareth has to do is glance at it for two seconds to know every word that's in it. To know they're listening in on your thoughts, watching you even when you're locked in a room. To have them appear and disappear, and never be sure whether they're really there or if you're just looking at one of Gareth's creations. To know that whatever job Gareth gives you to do, he could do it better and easier. No, of course you can't understand!"

He muttered an oath and, putting his knife away, pushed his way through the thorny bushes, relishing the feel of his skin being torn, revelling in the delight of making contact with a truly tangible object. Zameth, but Cole would regret letting him live!

He felt a hand on his shoulder, soft but firm, for just an instant. Catlike, he turned upon Alutha, his face still contorted with hatred.

"I'm sorry," she said, meeting his gaze. "I shouldn't have mentioned it."

"That's all right," he said. "He let me live. *That's* his weakness, and he'll pay for it. He'll pay for it in blood."

"I hope you're right," said Alutha.

"I am," he said firmly. "I've hurt his creatures twice; I can do it again."

"But have you hurt Cole?"

"You still don't understand: those creatures *are* Gareth Cole, or at least a part of him.'

"But if what you told me was true you killed dozens of them with Elston and my father, and yet he was able to defeat you."

"There's a way," he said grimly. "There's got to be a way. I'll find it.'

"I wish I had your confidence," she said honestly.

"You don't need it," he replied. "He's always left the Normans'—Normals'—women alone. I imagine he'll keep on doing so. And once I take care of Craston, you'll be a Baroness again. There's worse things to be."

"Not many," she said softly.

"What are you talking about?"

"I'm talking about being a Baroness," she said, slapping at a mosquito.

"What's wrong with that?"

"You object to being a pawn, don't you?" she asked, her eyes flashing with sudden fury. "Well, so do I. Why do you think Michael Drake married me? For my beauty? Take a good look at me. I have. I know what I am: the very plain daughter of a very powerful man. What have I got to offer a man? Sex? Charm? Beauty? Warmth? Whatever it is he craves, he can do better elsewhere. Unless he craves a Barony, as Michael did—and as you do. I know it, and my father knew it too. You see, it wasn't just a one-sided game on Michael's part. Oh, no, nothing so simple as that. My father rejected many a suitor until he found one with the proper capabilities—and lack of them—to make a proper son-in-law. He wanted an honest man, which Michael was, and a good general, which Michael also was. But to balance that he also wanted a man who didn't have the intellect and patience to outmaneuver him in the Council of Barons, as Elston might have done, or with the personality to rally the masses behind him. Michael filled the bill, and so I was given to Michael. And of course he had no use for me from the moment the marriage vows were spoken. I was a prisoner in my own house, unable to descend to the ground for fear that Michael might have me assassinated, afraid to go to the third floor for fear his mistresses might kill me.

"And now," she concluded, "I shall have to undergo the same thing again with you. With one exception."

"And what is that?" he asked.

"Since you'll possess considerably more power than Michael ever did, you'll be able to have me killed much sooner."

Donahoe did not reply to that, and they walked on in silence for another hour, until night fell. Then they camped by a stream, slaking their thirst and sitting up against a huge tree.

"There's one thing I don t understand," she said hesitantly as they stared across the water into the marsh beyond.

"What?" grunted the redbeard.

"It's been more than a week since we escaped from Craston's men, and you haven't touched me."

"Do you want me to?"

"No," she said, shuddering involuntarily at the thought. "But I expected you to. After all, there's no one around to make you keep your promise."

"If I were to rape you, you'd probably run away. And if you ran away, it might take me months to hunt you down—if you were still alive. No, raping you would be the surest way of preventing our marriage."

"And you wouldn't want to do that, would you?" she said bitterly.

"No, I wouldn't. I won you and all that goes with you." She was silent, and he continued. "And no one is going to take what's mine away from me. Unless . . ." He paused, scrutinizing her features.

"Unless what?" she asked uneasily.

"Unless you've got a lover hidden away somewhere who's waiting for me to return to the Hub so he can slip a knife between my ribs."

"You've nothing to fear on that account," she said. "I have no lover."

"Maybe an old one," he grunted.

"I've never had a lover."

"Haven't you ever wanted one?" he asked, curious.

114

"Yes. Once."

"What happened to him?"

"He died."

"How?"

"You killed him a long time ago," said Alutha Drake. She rolled over onto her side and closed her eyes. A minute later she was asleep, dreaming about a godlike young man who had once caught a foolish girl in his arms and laughingly set her back on her feet.

When she awoke he was gone. For a moment she was panic-stricken, but then she heard him walking through the underbrush. A few seconds later he broke into the clearing and began approaching her, holding something she couldn't quite make out in his hands.

"Where were you?" she asked, the fear of being left alone to die slowly leaving her.

"I brought you some blackberries," he said.

CHAPTER EIGHTEEN

"So you still think he'll be coming back to the Hub?" said Rysler, happy that for once the meeting was in his own luxurious quarters rather than in Craston's cramped, darkened rooms. Of all the Barons, only Craston refused to live in a castle, preferring to keep his apartments at the center of the city, and Rysler deeply resented the lack of Baronial splendor, despite the fact that he knew Craston was unable to appreciate the beauty of a castle.

"Of course," replied the blind Baron. "The problem we face is what to do with him after we capture him. Obviously he must be destroyed, and quickly, but I keep wondering if we can gain any useful information from him first. It would be risky, to be sure; every minute that he lives is risky to us. Yet it might well serve a useful purpose if we were to incarcerate him briefly in your dungeons once again."

"I don't see the risk involved," said Rysler. "After all, even if he does possess Elston's and Aldan's Baronies, they're momentarily worthless until he actually takes power. But on the other hand, we've tried to get information out of him before with no success. I don't know why this time should be any different."

"We're armed with a little more knowledge this time around," replied Craston. "For instance, I think we can safely assume that Donahoe told you the truth about the battle in the subways. Therefore, we know that Cole's mental monsters can occasionally be hurt, perhaps even killed. We can also assume that, much as Donahoe would like to kill Cole, he hasn't yet found a method of so doing. Similarly, we can assume that he's not going to find that method very soon or Cole would have destroyed him."

"I don't know," said Rysler dubiously. "Cole never bothers us in the Hub. Maybe we ought to just stay here and stop trying to invade the subways. We've already lost Michael, Elston and Aldan since capturing Donahoe; why risk any more?"

"Fool!" snapped Craston, smashing his fist into the arm of his chair. "Don't you realize yet that the one thing we *can't* do is sit still? Donahoe will be back any day now to claim at least two Baronies, possibly three —and Cole is still breeding his damned army. We've got to kill Donahoe, and we've got to try to demolish Cole's mutants while there's still a possibility that he can be beaten."

"There's one thing that has always puzzled me," said Rysler. "If Cole is half as powerful as he seems, what's holding him back? Why doesn't he conquer the world, if that's his goal? Why did he once steal our women and breed them to his mutants?"

"If I knew the answers to even one of those questions," said Craston, "I could probably bring about Gareth Cole's total defeat within forty-eight hours. But I don't know. Nobody does. All we can do is interpret his motives as best we can and keep trying to thwart him."

"Fat lot of good it's done us," muttered Rysler.

"Stop feeling sorry for yourself, Gerald," said Craston sharply. "You're not coming out of this in bad shape and you know it. In fact, once we get our hands on Donahoe and Alutha Drake, you'll be twice as powerful as you were two months ago." Rysler said nothing, and the blind Baron continued. "Now, what steps have you taken to apprehend Donahoe?"

"I've got a number of scouting parties scattered around the Hub, within about a fifty-mile radius," said Rysler. "I don't think he'll be able to get through, but if he does, I've also posted permanent guards around my castle, Drake's castle and your dwellings."

"You'd better post them around Elston's and Aldan's castles too," suggested Craston. "After all, they're as much his property as Drake's is. And don't forget—he's got Alutha with him. She'll have enough brains not to go back to her own castle."

"You know," began Rysler slowly, "all these plans and preparations are based on the assumption that Alutha Drake is still alive and with him. What if she's not? What if she's run away, or if he's killed her?"

"I hadn't seriously considered it," said Craston thoughtfully. "I presumed that Alutha probably had to tell him of the political situation to save her life, and that once told he would do everything in his power to protect her. However, even if I'm wrong and she *is* either dead or missing, I think we can still expect a visit from Donahoe. After all, even if he doesn't know she was Aldan's daughter, he does know that he is Michael's legal successor."

"And what if Donahoe is dead too?" asked Rysler.

"He's not," said Craston.

"What makes you so certain?" demanded Rysler.

"Ah, Gerald," sighed Craston. "You disappoint me so. Haven't you yet realized that the only real danger you and I must face is when we try to kill him?"

"That's ridiculous!" snorted Rysler. "No single man, not even Donahoe, can possibly present a threat to our forces."

"The threat will not come from Donahoe," said Craston contemptuously. "Poor blind Gerald. *It will come from Gareth Cole.*"

118

CHAPTER NINETEEN

"They'll be waiting for us, you know."

"I know," grunted the redbeard, pausing atop a small hill and scanning the overgrown countryside.

"You'd be smarter to give the whole thing up right now."

"And let a handful of Normals frighten me out of being a Baron?" He spat into the wind.

"Before you speak so condescendingly of us Normals," said Alutha, leaning against a tree, "have you ever considered the possibility that you might be one of us?"

"*Me?*" He threw back his head and roared with laughter.

"I mean it," she said. "I don't care who your parents were. Take a good look at yourself. You're physically normal in every way."

"So is Gareth," he reminded her.

"But Gareth has other powers," she countered. "What are yours?"

"I don't know."

"How old are you?"

"I'm not sure. Around thirty, I guess. Maybe a little older."

"If you had any extranormal powers, don't you think you'd know what they were by now?"

"It sounds logical enough," he admitted, "but they say Gareth didn't know about *his* powers until he was fully grown."

"That's not true," said Alutha. "He knew about them when he was much younger. He kept them a secret, but he knew. You haven't any powers. You're one of us."

"I don't know," he said slowly, scratching his head. "I don't know."

"Think about it."

"I am thinking about it," he said irritably. "Look, if I'm really a Normal, how in Rath did I get into the tunnels in the first place?"

"You're probably as much a freak of birth as Gareth was," she said. "My guess is that you're a throwback, a genetic freak of sorts. Normal people produced Gareth Cole; mutants produced you."

"I'm no freak!" he thundered. "Gareth is the freak, not me!"

"I didn't mean that," she apologized. "What I meant was—"

"I know what you meant," he interrupted. "It's just that I'm kind of touchy about the subject. I'm sorry I yelled at you."

Her eyes widened perceptibly, and a curious expression came over her face.

"What's the matter?" he demanded.

"Nothing," she said, smiling suddenly. "Nothing at all."

"Then why did you look like that?"

"Like what?"

"Surprised."

"That was the first time since we've been together that you've apologized for anything," said Alutha. "I'm flattered."

He uttered a growl of disgust and resumed his scrutiny of the countryside. A few minutes later he turned back to her again.

"So I'm a Normal?"

She nodded.

"I've fought them all my life," he said in agonized tones. "I've killed them wherever I've found them. I don't want to be a Normal. I hate Normals!"

"Some of us are worthwhile."

"Stramm was," he said, staring down at the ground. "Stramm was a good man, even though he captured me." He paused. "Gareth didn't have to kill him. He could have let him live. He couldn't do Gareth any harm." His fists tightened. He was working himself into a killing rage, as he did whenever he thought about Gareth Cole. "Damn it! Stramm was decent to me, he really was. And then I led him into the tunnels, and in two seconds he was gone. Just gone! No corpse, no bones, no ashes, nothing!" He bellowed a curse. "When I get my hands on him, so help me I'll rip him apart! I'll . . ." His fury became so great that he lapsed into incoherency. A minute later he paused for breath. Then, his composure partially regained, he turned to Alutha. "I don't want to be a Normal," he said in steady tones. "I hope I'm not. But if I am, that gives me one more reason to kill him."

"You have more than enough reasons," she replied. "What you need is a method."

"I know," he said, suddenly deflated. "I know I do. I'm getting close to it. I hurt his blasted creatures. Someday I'll know how to hurt him too."

"Don't hold your breath," she said.

"That's another reason I don't want to be a Normal," he snapped. "No gumption."

"All the gumption in the world is no substitute for realism."

"Zameth! Maybe Gareth ought to kill off the lot of you after all! Where's your guts, woman?"

"Stramm had guts, as you so quaintly put it," said Alutha. "So did my father. Where did it get them?"

He growled something unintelligible and started walking again. With a sigh Alutha fell into step behind him. When they had gone a little more than a mile she suddenly reached out and grabbed his arm.

121

"What is it now?" he demanded.

"Something's wrong!" she said in an urgent half-whisper.

"What are you talking about?" he said, lowering his voice to a whisper too.

"I don't know," she replied. "It's just a feeling."

"What is?"

"Don't go this way."

"Why not?"

"I don't know. I just feel apprehensive."

"All right, my courageous Normal Baroness. Which way do *you* think we should go?"

"I don't know. To the left, perhaps."

"Bah! You see ghosts and gremlins in every shadow!"

He began walking in his original direction. Before he had gone another half mile he heard voices directly ahead of him. Motioning Alutha to retreat, he withdrew his warclub and crept ahead.

Now he could see them: four Normal warriors, all sitting in the shade of a giant tree.

"This is the craziest wild goose chase I've ever been on," one was saying. "Even if he's in the area, I'd say the chances of our finding any sign of him are a thousand to one."

"At least," added another, taking a long drink from his canteen.

"Maybe we should go back and tell Baron Rysler that we haven't seen any trace of him," said the first warrior. "What do you say, Edward?"

But Edward was past the point of ever saying anything again, for the redbeard had snaked his way through the bushes and crushed his skull with a single blow of his warclub.

A second Normal was dead before the remaining pair even realized that Donahoe was in their midst. Their moment of realization was brief; a moment later both of them lay motionless on the ground.

Donahoe went back down the trail for Alutha. "You were right!" he panted. "Damned lucky guess. What gave them away?"

"I don't understand," she said.

"What did you see back there? I'm a pretty good man on a trail, but whatever it was, I missed it."

"It was just a feeling. Somehow I just felt very scared."

He shrugged. "Well, there's nothing to be afraid of now. They're all dead."

"I imagined they would be."

"Don't start feeling sorry for them. They would have killed us if they'd had the chance."

"I know."

"Or is it that you think I'm a murderer again?"

"No. Honestly I don't. I just don't like killing, no matter who's right or wrong."

"Then tell your Normal friends to stop hunting me."

"They're hunting me too," she reminded him.

He took a long, deep breath, then released it. "I know." He looked at her and his expression softened. "I guess it hasn't been any easier for you than for me."

"No, it hasn't."

"Nothing we can do about it now."

"I know. It all seems so futile, though. Running away for weeks, killing our own people, just so that we can go back to the Hub to be murdered."

"What do you want me to do—live in this damned forest for the rest of my life?"

"No, of course not."

"Well then?" He glared at her expectantly.

"There are other Normal cities. Why not go to one of them?"

"If I decided not to go to the Hub, I wouldn't have to keep you alive any longer," he said. "You know that, don't you?"

"Yes," she said softly. "I know that. But I'm not asking that you remain there forever."

"How long then?"

"Just until Andrew has gotten over his fervor for killing you."

"*His* fervor? Zameth! The whole damned city is out to kill me! Every last one of them thinks I murdered Stramm and your father."

"I'd forgotten," she admitted. "Andrew is the only one who wants me dead, and I'd gotten in the habit of thinking that the same applied to you."

"It doesn't," he said brusquely. "Now that that's settled, let's get going."

They headed back toward the Hub, but when they reached the spot where he had encountered the warriors, only three bodies remained. The redbeard mouthed a curse and turned to Alutha.

"Damn! I could have sworn they were all dead!"

"They are," she said, surveying the carnage.

"No they're not. There was a fourth one."

"Where is he?"

"I don't know," said the redbeard, "but if he lives long enough to reach any other patrols, this place is going to be crawling with Normals before long."

"What are you going to do?" she asked.

"I'm not sure," he said, rubbing his bearded chin vigorously. "I'd like to go on to the Hub, but they'll be waiting for us behind every bush and every tree along the way."

"We can go to one of the other cities."

"And throw away the chance to be a Baron? Not on your life! We'll live in the fields for a few more weeks and then take another crack at getting into the Hub." He paused. "Unless . . ."

"Unless what?"

"Unless you'll agree to go through with a formal marriage ceremony the minute we get to another city," he said. "That would make it official, and Craston and

Rysler would have to turn over Drake's and Povich's property to me. Is it a deal?"

Her first inclination was to refuse. Drake was bad enough, but the thought of being wed to this barbarian, to feel his huge calloused hands roaming over her flesh, to know that she was once again a piece of physical and political property to be forgotten the instant her purpose was served, was intolerable. It was only when she considered the alternatives that she realized that they were equally repugnant. If she refused to marry him he would either approach the Hub and get both of them killed on the spot, or else they would lead this hideous existence in the forest for an uncertain amount of time, after which she would be forced into marriage with him anyway.

Neither of her choices would lead to an enviable position, but marrying him now would put the threat to her safety out of the immediate future, and given enough time she might conceivably find some means of manipulating him.

"Yes, it's a deal," she said at last.

CHAPTER TWENTY

They were married neither quickly nor easily.

They marched south for about a week, in the general direction of Kingston, which had become an almost totally agrarian society, surrounded by farms and fields where once there had been brick and concrete. Kingston seemed an ideal site to the redbeard, far enough removed from Craston and the Hub so that he need expect no trouble from the blind Baron, and close enough to the tunnels for him to reach Cole's domain in a hard two-day march.

The roads leading to the isolated community were overgrown from lack of use, and it was on one of these that he encountered one of the very few wild beasts that still roamed the countryside. Most of the area's fauna, of which no great quantity existed to begin with, had been killed during the bygone war. The handful that survived had evidently suffered violent genetic damage or mutation, for all but a very small number of species had died out centuries ago. Members of the cat family seemed to bear up under the radiation better than most other animals, and the sudden imbalance between predator and prey caused most of the cats to cannibalize or starve.

It had been a bobcat of sorts that attacked Donahoe as he walked the ancient road with Alutha. He killed it quickly enough with his warclub, but not before it slashed open his forearm with its claws. The wound was superficial, but though the redbeard protested Alutha insisted upon tending to it. She got some clear water from a nearby creek, and a moment later her fingers were working nimbly away at the gashes, cleansing them out and binding them. It was the closest she had ever voluntarily been to him, and it was all he could do to refrain from ripping her clothes off and raping her on the spot. As she applied the finishing touches to the primitive dressing he feigned discomfort and jerked his hand away. It brushed against her breast and lingered there for a few seconds before he withdrew it. If she had any inkling that he had moved his hand for any reason other than pain she gave no indication of it, except to work more rapidly.

When she finished with the wound she stepped away quickly. "How does it feel now?" she asked.

"Fine. I told you before that it didn't need any treatment. Rath! I've survived a lot worse things than this!"

"Swords are usually pretty clean," she replied. "A wildcat's talons aren't. Most of them are carrion eaters."

"So what?"

"They like their food to be high."

"I don't understand," said the redbeard.

"They don't eat their kills right away. Depending on what type of cat it is, he'll either bury it in the ground or drag it up a tree and wedge the corpse of his victim between a couple of branches. Then he'll leave it alone for anywhere from five days to two weeks. When the meat gets properly high—rotten enough to suit his taste —he'll come back for it."

"What's all this got to do with me?" asked the redbeard.

"The meat is rotten, spoiled. He'll dig his claws into it to hold it still while he's tearing away chunks of it with his teeth. Some of the flesh will adhere to the claws, getting higher ever day, until after a couple of weeks those claws have much the same effect as a poisoned arrow. If I hadn't cleaned out your wound, some residue from the claws would doubtless have infected the scratches and ultimately gotten into your bloodstream and killed you. Does that answer your question?"

127

"I guess you may have saved my life."

"You can thank me by keeping your hands off my body," replied Alutha, her dark eyes flashing in the sunlight, "or next time I'll leave you here to die."

"I don't know what you're talking about," lied the redbeard.

"You know exactly what I'm talking about," she shot back. "Just see to it that it doesn't happen again."

"It won't—until we're married. Then it's my body as much as yours. Would you like to hear what I'm going to do to it then?"

"No." Coldly.

"You might like it."

"I couldn't care less what you do to me, murderer. I made a political bargain and I'll stick by it, but don't ever, even for an instant, demand or expect me to like it."

"We'll see about that," grinned the redbeard, stretching himself and once again taking up their trek. She joined him, and they walked side by side in silence for the remainder of the day. They camped by the bank of a small stream and recommenced their journey just after daybreak.

Donahoe was feeling good. Not high-spirited, but healthier and fitter than he'd been in years. He hadn't had a drink of anything stronger than water since before leading the attack on the tunnels, and it had been even longer since he had smoked a pipe or cigar, or, he added with a mental wince, bedded a woman. He missed all three, the drinking and the smoking and especially the women, but he found that he now possessed considerably more stamina, and his perpetual morning cough was gone. Yes, he was healthier, though one could safely say that he was far from happier.

He had changed in other ways too. It would be incorrect to say that he now felt compassion for another human being, but he did feel some concern for Alutha's comfort, partially because he was intent upon protecting his political future and partially for reasons he did not and never would fully understand or even acknowledge. Also, he was more prone to thinking than previously. The mind that had usually remained blank except on those extremely rare occasions when it was forced to function at a primitive level now was constantly flooded with thought. Not deep, philosophic questions and answers, for Donahoe was neither concerned with such things nor capable of dealing with them, but he did manage to conjure up a never-ending stream of plans for murdering Gareth Cole, and even tossed in a mental picture or two of how he intended to rub the Hub once he got rid of Craston and Rysler.

Thus it was that he was able to walk in utter silence for hours, which was accepted with gratitude by Alutha Drake. Somehow, every conversation they had either ended with the redbeard cursing Gareth Cole or gleefully predicting their wedding night. Both were equally distasteful to her, and the less they spoke the better she liked it. She no longer feared him, but she intended to avoid intercourse with him, whether social or sexual, for as long as possible. She felt a certain sympathy for him, a sympathy approaching pity, when she considered the absolute hell his life must have been in Gareth Cole's subways; but, she mentally added, all the sympathy in the world couldn't excuse the hideous crimes he had committed against the Normals. And especially against one particular Normal man, many long years ago when she had foolishly believed the world was as innocent as she was.

Donahoe's wound had healed before they reached Kingston, and he entered the city feeling quite fit and healthy. No notice was taken of him and Alutha, and he surmised that Kingston had become a stopover for travelers between the Hub and the more southerly Normal cities. They were directed to a boarding house where, to keep up the pretense of being a married couple, he rented out a single room. She sat in a chair all that night, refusing to join him in the bed. After a brief argument, he shrugged and rolled over, and was snoring a moment later.

Morning found him considerably refreshed, and eager to make plans for his future. Since that future very definitely included Alutha Drake, he included her in his conversation. Not that he would have needed her to converse with; long years in the tunnels had made him quite adept at talking to himself. But having some-one else to speak with was a distinct advantage.

"Well," he began, "I suppose the first thing to do is get married. The sooner that's over with the better."

"You're wrong, Will," she said calmly. "The first thing to do is find a way of getting some money. You're not living on Stramm's estate any longer. You'll have to pay for the wedding, and sooner or later you'll have to pay for this room as well."

"I hadn't even thought about that," he admitted. He paused, then added, "Why don't we just tell them you're Baroness Drake? That ought to get us a little credit."

"That's the most foolish suggestion you've come up with yet," she said contemptuously. "What if they know Craston is looking for you? We haven't been recognized yet, but that is no assurance they don't know about you."

"They may be after me, but they'll leave you alone. You're a Baroness, remember?"

"That's precisely why they *won't* leave me alone, if Craston's been in contact with them. If I die, there's another Barony up for grabs."

"Since you're the one with all the ideas," he said sullenly, "why don't *you* figure out how we're going to get some money."

"You could always work for it."

130

"I'm a general," he snapped. "Generals don't work for wages."

"They do if they're hungry," she retorted. "And you're not a general any longer, in case you've forgotten."

"That's right. I'm a Baron."

"Barons can starve just as easily as generals," she said coldly.

He glowered at her for a moment. "All right, I'll get your damned money!" he said. "Just be ready for one Rath of a wedding night when I get back!"

He stalked out of the room and left the building. For a moment he thought of returning lest she run away while he was gone, but he decided not to. Her reasons for keeping her identity a secret were valid. She knew he would kill or expose her if she tried to double-cross him, and if death was preferable to matrimony she would have taken her own life weeks ago. Satisfied, he walked out into the dirt streets of Kingston.

While the area was primarily agricultural, a handful of shops and stores had sprung up of necessity. It was toward these that he headed, though not with the intention of asking for work. What he had wanted in the past, he had taken; he saw no reason why this should be any different. Also, he placed less stock in currency than the Normals, since he had never needed it in the tunnels. Hence, the thought of depriving a store of its money seemed no more serious an offense than picking fruit from a field without seeking out the farmer to pay for it.

He picked a likely looking store, one that dealt in clothing and fabrics, and entered it. A moment's observation told him that the money was kept in a small box behind a counter toward the rear of the shop. He browsed over the goods, slowly moving in the direction of the money box, until he was the only customer in the shop. Then he leisurely withdrew his warclub and brandished it at the proprietor.

"Give me that box," he said calmly, pointing toward the object in question.

The proprietor scrutinized him, decided that he was both serious and likely to emerge victorious if a fight were to ensue, and yielded up the money.

"If you say a word about this to anyone," said Donahoe, "I'll come back and split you open from top to bottom."

With that he turned and left the shop. He half-expected to hear the man he had just robbed scream for help, but the interior of the store remained silent. Convinced that his parting threat had accomplished its purpose, he walked directly and openly back to the boarding house, making no attempt to hide his trail through a more circuitous route.

Upon arriving, he found Alutha asleep in the bed. Shaking her into wakefulness, he displayed the contents of the box to her. She was about to ask where he had gotten it when a commotion from down the street took their attention. Donahoe took a quick look out the window and saw a large group of armed men walking toward his quarters. Leading them was the shop-owner he had just robbed.

"Zameth!" he said furiously. "That son of a bitch! I warned him not to say anything!"

"Is he the man you stole the money from?" asked Alutha.

The redbeard nodded his head. "We've got to get out of here, and fast. There are too damned many of them, even for me."

He picked up the box and walked to the door.

"Leave the money, Will," said Alutha, following him.

"Leave it? Are you crazy?"

"We won't need it if we're on the run, and if you leave it behind, it may satisfy them. Unless you relish the thought of being chased day and night."

132

He stared indecisively at the box for a moment, then hurled it onto the bed. Grabbing her arm, he opened the door and walked out into the adjoining hallway.

"There must be a back entrance here somewhere," he said. "Let's try to find it."

Find it he did, and in a matter of minutes they were safely beyond the city limits. They walked all day and part of the night before he was convinced that they were safe from pursuit. Then, at last, he allowed them the luxury of a rest, setting up a camp in a small clearing.

"Word of this will get back to Craston, you know," said Alutha, sitting down and supporting her back against the bole of an ancient maple tree.

"Like Rath it will! Do you think Craston is informed of every theft that takes place hundreds of miles away?"

"Yes, if it's committed by Red Will Donahoe."

"How will he know it was me?" scoffed the redbeard.

"If you shaved your beard off, you'd have a point," she replied, brushing a fallen inchworm from her hair, "but until you do so, you have, to put it mildly, a rather unique appearance. Unique enough for word of it to get back to Andrew."

"So what if it does?" he shrugged. "It'll be weeks before he hears of it."

"Possibly," she countered, "but you're a famous man, Will—the greatest murderer in Gareth Cole's living arsenal. Other people will recognize your description, too. In fact, I'd be willing to bet that every man, woman and child in Kingston knows who you are by now."

"It was that damned shopkeeper's fault! If he'd just kept his mouth shut . . ."

"If you hadn't robbed him he wouldn't have had anything to talk about."

"We needed money," he said. "You were the one who told me to go out and get it."

"I told you to go out and *work* for it," she countered.

"There's a big difference."

"To you," he said, closing the subject. "By the way, what makes you so sure they'll know who I am? Nobody recognized me yesterday."

"You didn't rob a store and threaten to kill a man yesterday," she said. "It takes people a while to put two and two together. They didn't recognize you as the famed mutant monster until you started acting like one."

"I'm no mutant!" he snapped. "And don't you forget it!"

"Don't behave like one," she replied, "and I'll find it much easier to remember."

He uttered an oath of exasperation, then tried changing the subject again. "Where to next?"

"I really don't know," said Alutha. "I imagine the whole Normal alliance will know our approximate whereabouts before long. I think we'd better remain in hiding until we can return safely to the Hub."

"I'm a Baron!" he snapped. "I'm not going to hole up like some wild animal, waiting for Craston to forget about us. We'll try another city."

"I suspect that any nearby city will be waiting for you," she pointed out.

"We'll enter by night."

"They'll find you in the morning. Besides, what good will it do to enter a city? It's easier to hide out here."

"We can't get married here," said the redbeard. "And that, in case it slipped your mind, is the reason you're still alive. Now, what city is nearest to us?"

"I don't remember the small ones," she said, "but I suppose we're not too far from Providence."

"We'll head for it first thing in the morning," he promised.

"If you insist," she said with a sigh. "But I think you're making a mistake."

"We'll see about that," he said confidently.

CHAPTER TWENTY-ONE

Andrew Craston sat alone in his dark, silent room. There was a knock at the door.

"Joshua?" he asked.

The door opened. "Yes, sir."

"Is he here?"

"Yes," replied Joshua.

"Firmly bound?"

"Yes."

"Has he been incarcerated long?"

"Two days, sir."

"I suppose that'll do," sighed Craston. "Bring him in."

A third man entered the room at swordpoint. He peered into the darkness, trying to locate Craston, but was unsuccessful. He was a large man, a huge man, bald and clean-shaven. He wore nothing but a pair of pants, held up by a rope woven of weeds and grasses. Two sets of chains held his arms behind his back, nor would Craston have been safe with a less secure binding.

"I'm told you were captured on our side of the river," said Craston after waiting for the man to become thoroughly uneasy. There was no answer, and Craston added, "I assume you're either nodding your head or shaking it negatively. I'm afraid you'll have to say your answers aloud. I'm quite blind."

Silence.

"I believe I asked you a question, prisoner," said Craston.

"You know the answer," came the calm reply. "Therefore, I feel no need of replying."

"All right," said the blind Baron. "I'll ask a question I don't know the answer to. What is your name?"

"Thurman."

"Is that a first name or a last name? What's the rest of it."

"Do you know anyone else named Thurman?" asked the man.

"No."

"Then my answer would seem to be sufficient."

"I get the feeling that I am losing control of this interview," grinned Craston, amused. "What were you doing on our side of the river?"

"Looking for something."

"Something—or some*one?*" said Craston quickly.

"If I had meant someone, I would have said it," replied Thurman.

"I believe you would have," admitted the blind Baron. "However, I am not accustomed to arrogance in my prisoners, nor do I tolerate it. We can easily continue our discussion as the torturers work on you, if that's what you want."

"It is of no import to me," said Thurman calmly.

"You may think differently after they begin."

"I doubt it. I am completely impervious to pain."

"Ah," said Craston, leaning back in his chair. "What other little things should I know about you?"

"Nothing that will be the slightest use to you."

"Joshua," said Craston. "Stick your sword into him. Not enough to kill him, but considerably more than enough to make him flinch." He waited in utter silence. "Have you done it yet?"

"Yes. Baron," said Joshua.

"Was there any reaction?"

"None, sir."

"Well," said the blind Baron, "it would seem you were telling the truth."

"I had no reason to lie," said Thurman, "since my statement would naturally inspire you to test its veracity."

"Naturally," agreed Craston. "Now then, what were

136

you looking for when you were captured?"

"I am not at liberty to say."

"And I don't imagine we can torture it out of you, can we?" said Craston.

"I don't imagine so," said Thurman.

"When was the last time you had any food or water?"

"Sometime last month," said Thurman, as calm as ever.

"I suppose we can't starve you into telling us that which you want to keep secret, can we?" queried Craston rhetorically.

"I very much doubt it," replied Thurman.

"How's Gareth feeling these days?" asked Craston, for lack of anything better to say.

"Not too well. He came down with a cold a few weeks ago, and it has lingered on."

"I don't suppose he'll die of it?"

"No, he won't."

"I find this a fruitless and frustrating discussion, Thurman. Do you get that feeling too?"

"It is of no importance to me."

"It should be, though," said Craston. "If I decide that you're of no value to me, I shall probably have you killed."

"Any other action would be totally illogical," agreed Thurman gravely.

"And the thought of dying doesn't bother you?"

"No. I am quite curious to experience the sensations of my consciousness leaving my body."

"It happens every time you go to sleep," said Craston. "Or don't you ever sleep either?"

"No, I never do."

"You never eat, you never sleep, you can't feel pain. You wouldn't be the end result of Gareth Cole's breeding program, would you?"

"No. Though he has never told me so, I suspect that I am a failure."

137

"And it doesn't bother you any more than the thought of death does?"

"Why should it? The failing is genetic, not of my own doing. Do you feel you are a failure because you are blind?"

"A point well taken," said Craston. "Joshua, how did you ever capture our friend here?"

"He stopped dead in his tracks when we yelled at him, and made no effort to hinder us when we put the chains on him," said Joshua.

"How strong are you, Thurman?" asked Craston. "Can you break your chains?"

"Not quite," admitted Thurman. "I tried once."

"Well, it appears very obvious that you wanted to be captured—or at least that Gareth wanted us to capture you. I don't suppose you'd like to tell me why?"

"I had never been in a Norman city. I was curious, so I allowed you to bring me here."

"I'm afraid I'll need a better answer than that," said Craston.

"I'm afraid you won't get one," said Thurman.

"Tell me, Thurman—can you see me?" asked the blind Baron.

"No."

"Does that upset you?"

"A little," said Thurman. "I like to see my inquisitors."

"How would you like to spend the rest of your life in a room even darker than this, chained to a wall with neither food nor drink nor company?"

"I don't think I'd like it at all."

"That's precisely what I intend to do with you if you don't respond more willingly to my questions."

"What must be, must be," said Thurman calmly.

Craston felt the keen edge of his temper beginning to cut through the cold exterior he had donned for the prisoner. He took a deep breath, held it while he shut his eyes and tried to clear his mind, then released it

138

and leaned forward in his chair.

"We'll try again," he announced to the two other occupants of the room. "Why were you on this side of the river? What were you doing away from the subways?"

"What are subways?" Thurman inquired politely.

"Tunnels, damn it!" yelled Craston. "What were you doing out of them?"

"I told you: looking for something."

"For what?"

"I have been forbidden to tell you," said Thurman patiently.

"Forbidden? By whom?"

"By Gareth, of course. Who else could forbid me to speak to you if I so desired?"

"True," said Craston. "Why doesn't Gareth want me to know what you were looking for?"

"I'm not at liberty to say."

"Of course not," said the blind Baron. "But it does stand to reason that Gareth either knew what you were looking for, or in fact may very well have sent you himself. Otherwise, he couldn't have forbidden you to speak about it with me, could he?"

"Your conclusions are most logical," said Thurman. "One of them is, in fact, quite correct."

"I'll assume he sent you," said Craston. "It seems far too irregular for you to have left the subways of your own accord." He paused, then continued while drumming his fingers against the arm of his wooden chair. "Gareth sent you, that much is clear. But what could he possibly have wanted you to look for?"

"I'm afraid I won't tell you," said Thurman.

"But you *will* permit me to use a little deductive reasoning, won't you?" said Craston with a cold smile. "Cole uses no objects other than his mind, Thurman. None of them could possibly be very important to him. I therefore submit that you were looking for the same thing I'm looking for—Donahoe."

"That's not so," said Thurman. "I told you, I was looking for . . ."

"I know what you told me!" snapped Craston. "I also know what you were looking for. And when you couldn't find him you came here, or rather allowed yourself to be taken here, in order to see if we had Donahoe. And, since I have no doubt that Gareth Cole is listening in on this little conversation right now, he knows that Donahoe isn't here. You've served your purpose, mutant, haven't you?"

"Yes, I have," said Thurman.

"And you could break those chains whenever you wished?"

"Certainly," said Thurman, flexing his huge biceps. The chains cracked and fell away.

"And now that you've done your duty, you intend to kill me and walk right out the door and return to the subways."

"I believe you have summed up the situation quite adequately," said Thurman, advancing upon him.

"Joshua!" yelled Craston. "Shut the door!"

He heard it slam an instant later and he arose from his chair, drawing his sword as he did so.

"You can't see in the dark," he said, fully as calm as Thurman. "Neither can I, of course, but I've lived the last twenty years in utter blackness. I know where you are, Thurman. I can hear you breathing, I can even smell the sweat on your body. You're a walking dead man. That door won't open again until you've taken your final gasp of air. Consider that, mutant, while you wait for the blow to fall."

He'd had a purpose in talking. He hoped for Thurman to advance upon him while his words muffled the mutant's movement. He suddenly fell silent, and in the instant that it took Thurman to react to his silence by a similar cessation of motion, his keen ears pinpointed the mutant's position. He approached slowly, his sword held high over his head. Then, when he was sure he was within easy reach, he brought it down with all the strength he could summon. Thurman fell like a rock.

"Joshua!"

The door opened and Joshua entered, holding a torch in his hand. "He's dead, Baron. His skull is split in two."

"Of course he's dead," said Craston irritably. "Just as Cole planned it."

"I'm afraid I don't follow you, sir," said Joshua, puzzled.

"There's something very wrong with this whole situation," said the blind Baron. "I know *what,* but I don't know *why.*"

"I really don't understand what you're talking about, Baron," said Joshua.

"Joshua, I usually give you credit for having more brains than Gerald. Now I wonder." Joshua just stared at him, and, hearing no response, Craston continued patiently. "Did it ever occur to you, Joshua, that Gareth Cole didn't need Thurman to search the Hub for Donahoe, that indeed he could have done so far more efficiently by sending a flock of his firebirds overhead?"

"I must admit it didn't, sir."

"It should have. Now, consider who—or what, if you prefer—he *did* send to us: an emotionless creature that possesses no physical feeling. He never hungers, he never thirsts, he can feel no pain. What does that imply to you?"

"Nothing," said Joshua, "except that he sent a man who couldn't be tortured into revealing secret information."

"Precisely. He sent us a sacrificial lamb, a man whose sole duty was to say what he said and then be killed by me in such a way that I would think my life really was in danger."

"You've lost me again, Baron," said Joshua, more perplexed than ever.

141

"You pinpointed it yourself, Joshua—he sent a man who couldn't be tortured into revealing secret information."

"But we got that information," protested Joshua.

"*I've* got it," said Craston, "but not from Thurman. Or at least, not directly. No one could trick or torture him into saying anything Gareth didn't want him to say. That would be paradoxical, since his very value lay in the fact that he could not be forced into anything."

"Do you mean to say that Gareth didn't send him here to look for Donahoe?"

"Of course not! Gareth sent him here to make us *think* Donahoe is nearby."

"Then he's not?"

"No. Cole tried to trick us into wasting our time around the Hub, while Donahoe prepares elsewhere."

"Prepares for what?" asked Joshua.

"I don't know. But it must be pretty damned important for Gareth Cole to go to all this trouble to keep us from looking for him."

"Then what's our next step?"

"I'm not sure," said the blind Baron. "We'll take the mutant's corpse back and leave it by the river with a defiant note pinned onto it. That's the kind of thing he'd expect us to do if his plan worked, and I wouldn't want to disappoint him. Then we'll try to figure out where Donahoe might be, and more important, what he might be preparing for."

"And that's all we have to go on, sir?"

"That's all. I wonder," he said, half to himself, "if even Donahoe really knows any more than that."

CHAPTER TWENTY-TWO

Providence had been completely passed over by the war. Or, rather, none of the bombs had struck the city proper. The radiation, however, had proved totally fatal to the entire populace, and before the city was inhabited again, a century later, most of its facilities had decayed. Those which remained in working order were unusable by the time the city dwellers realized their purposes.

Thus Providence was a living anachronism, a structure of steel and brick and concrete which was inhabited by people who understood nothing of its various parts and even less of the whole. Originally a mere handful of twenty peasant farmers had emigrated to Providence. The city's entire populace, with less than one hundred exceptions, were the descendants of the original twenty. Their numbers had grown slowly, and even now only two thousand men and women lived in the city. A larger population might have made capital of the mechanical treasures of the long-dead metropolis, but no crops could grow through the concrete and they had always been forced to return to the land, living in the city by night and working the fields bordering the city by day. Craston knew of the situation in Providence, as had the other Barons, but all were at a loss to explain why it hadn't evolved in the same manner as the Hub. Explanations were purely academic, though; the existence of the city and its current condition were irrefutable facts.

Many blocks, ancient and crumbling, were completely deserted. Others were in temporary disuse. The earliest settlers evidently possessed no knowledge of the written word, for most of the libraries were empty, their contents having been burned to provide heat during the first few winters. Where windows had been broken, the apartments were empty, the residents having moved their belongings to a residence in better repair.

The street lighting, once fully automated to coincide with the fall of darkness, no longer functioned, and hence Donahoe and Alutha were able to walk unseen down some of the major thoroughfares. The redbeard, ill at ease whenever he felt encased either in a room, a tunnel or now a city, quickened his pace. His steps echoed throughout the area, but there was no one around to challenge him, and before long he and Alutha had found a small apartment building that suited Donahoe's needs. The walls were crumbling, the windows were broken or completely absent, and the staircase had huge gaping holes in it. He was certain that no one would think of looking for them there, when there were so many better places available.

They slept, unbothered, until shortly after daybreak. Then Donahoe instructed Alutha to remain there while he sought out a man who had the necessary legal power to make him Povich's successor as well as Drake's.

The city, even the inhabited portions, was empty, the great majority of the tiny populace having already left to work in the fields. Mindful of what had happened in Kingston, Donahoe elected to loot an apartment rather than burglarize a store. Then, with a wad of money tucked beneath his belt, he continued his search.

For two hours he walked the dead streets of Providence, looking for some sign of life. Once he thought he heard a small child crying, but he was unable to trace the sound to its source and soon gave up trying. By the time the sun was directly overhead he began to get hungry and plundered another apartment. This one had a side of meat hanging in the bathroom, and it suddenly occurred to him how very long it had been since he had eaten anything except fruit and vege-

144

tables. He examined the meat, smelled it, decided it wasn't yet rotten, and cut off a large slab of it with his dagger. He then wrapped it in a small window curtain and prepared to take it back to Alutha with him. He had eaten raw meat a few times in the past, and while he would do so again if the occasion demanded, he preferred not to. Somehow he and Alutha would find a way to set an undetected fire, and with that thought firmly embedded in his mind, he left the building, planning to return immediately to the apartment where he had left her.

He had walked almost three blocks before the realization dawned upon him that he was completely lost.

Quickly he surveyed his surroundings. A few street signs still remained, fossil holdovers from a long-dead age, but he knew with a sickening sensation in his stomach that he hadn't bothered to note the street upon which Alutha awaited him. The numbers on the buildings were meaningless to him; he still did not know their purpose, though he now recalled that his own building had also possessed a four-digit number.

He glanced up at the sky. It was still midday, but he could make no closer approximation than that. How long he had walked, how rapidly he had walked, from what direction he had approached, all were questions to which he could supply no answers.

He tried to consider the consequences of his act. He himself could remain safe indefinitely, of that he was sure. He had only to hide in the more dilapidated areas of the city by night to avoid detection, and if he never stole food from the same section of town twice in a row it might be weeks, even months, before the townspeople knew they had an unwanted visitor in their midst.

But Alutha was a different story. She had no reason to wait for him if Craston's agents hadn't yet notified the city that she was to be destroyed. And even if she wanted to await his return, she was without food and probably without water. He knew that he could not have waited for much more than two days under such conditions; he gave her until nightfall. Then she would go out in search of nourishment.

His mind continued functioning in its slow, painfully laborious way, seeking a solution to his problem. For the first time in his life he found himself in awe of someone besides Gareth Cole. He wished that he were either Craston or Stramm; surely there must be a simple answer, one they would see in an instant.

But he wasn't Stramm or Craston. Stramm was dead and Craston was hunting him down with all the resources of a Baron of the Hub. He was Red Will Donahoe, and he didn't need any Normal to hold his hand and show him the way to find Alutha. He mouthed a curse and set his mind to work once again.

He could search through the city for months without finding the apartment. That much was painfully clear. And even if he found it in a few days, there was no assurance Alutha would be there; in fact, there was every reason to believe that she wouldn't be. Therefore, searching for the apartment would be useless.

Well then, what was the next step? She would leave the building for food, of course. Where would she go? He spat on the ground. How in Rath could he know where she'd go if he didn't know where she was starting out from? The only thing he could be sure of was that she'd avoid the center of town and try to steal a meal from a nearby apartment while—

Wait a minute! The redbeard's whole body tensed as a new observation flashed across his mind. She would be getting hungry just when the farmers came home, and she'd stay hidden inside the building until darkness blanketed the city. But then all the apartments with food would be filled. She couldn't go to any of them with impunity as he'd been able to do during the day. In fact, she would have to do just the reverse—she would have to avoid all the habitable apartments and rob a store!

What store? He didn't know, but he hadn't passed any during his morning trek. Therefore, it seemed safe to assume there were none in the immediate vicinity of her apartment.

"And if I were starving and could only get a meal by robbing a food store, where would I look for it?" he said aloud. "In the center of town, where I would guess most of the businesses would be located!"

The next question was obvious: exactly where was the center of town? He had no way of knowing, but again he tried to place himself in Alutha's shoes. Never having been to Providence before, she too would be unacquainted with the city's layout. How would she hit upon the proper place to find her store? He looked around him. Obviously he was in a residential district. How did he know? The same way she would know: the size of the buildings. Yes, he told himself with a growing sense of excitement, that *had* to be it—the larger the buildings, the closer he was to the heart of the city.

He began his search for the ancient skyscrapers immediately. Not from anxiety, for he was not at all sure his reasoning, though sound, would prove correct, but because he was more likely to be recognized if he stayed where he was. The business district of a deserted city would offer numerous places of concealment, whereas if he remained here he would run the risk of bumping into a returning farmer when he finally went searching for Alutha.

In an hour he drew within sight of a number of huge buildings, and another half hour found him hiding in an alleyway that afforded him a perfect view of a large intersection, one which possessed a pair of food markets.

Soon the sun began dipping low in the west, and before long a few farmers began crossing through the downtown area, headed for home after a hard day's work. Then it was dark, and once again the streets were deserted.

Donahoe began counting to himself to kill time. When he reached ten thousand he decided he had been wrong and got ready to leave in search of a place to spend the night. Then he heard her.

The footsteps came slowly and hesitantly at first; then, as she became convinced that there was no one around to see her, they became faster and surer. A moment later she strode into his line of vision and he stepped out to greet her.

"Will!" she said, shocked by his sudden appearance. "I was sure they had found you!"

"They didn't. Nobody knows we're here."

"Where were you? Why didn't you come back? I waited all day for you."

"I had my reasons," he said gruffly, unwilling to appear a fool in her eyes. "I have food. Let's go."

"All right," she said. "But I must admit I don't know how to get back to our rooms."

"It's not important. We'll change locations every night until we're ready to leave. The Normals are too damned stupid to figure that out. When they find one of our apartments, they'll wait for us there until Rath freezes over."

"Did you find the man you were looking for?" she asked after they had walked in silence for a few blocks.

"Not yet, but I will. I have money now."

"How did you get it?" she asked him.

"I got it," was his only answer.

For three more nights they shifted from slum to slum, abandoning each in the middle of the day. The redbeard tried to sneak up on some of the Normals, to overhear their conversations and see if they knew of him yet, but they seemed never to leave their homes after dark, and he dared not approach them in the daylight.

Then, on the fourth evening, as he was going back to the center of town to pilfer some more food, he bumped into a man as he rounded a corner. The fellow fell to the ground, then stood up and was about to rebuke the redbeard when suddenly his mouth fell agape.

"My God!" he yelled. "It's Donahoe!" He turned and ran down the street, screaming Donahoe's name at the top of his lungs.

The redbeard debated going after him and silencing him, then decided that the damage had already been done and headed off for Alutha at a run. He arrived half an hour later, explained what had happened to her between gasps of air, and went back into the street to see if he had been followed. The coast was clear, and he went back upstairs to his room.

"They'll be looking for us now, Will," she said. "They know who you are, and I'm sure Craston has placed a high price on your head."

"Nothing's changed," he replied. "Providence is a big city. They won't know where to begin looking."

"Yes they will," she said. "They'll empty every apartment of food and put it all in a single place. They'll force us to come after it, and they'll be waiting for us. They won't have to look, Will."

"It'll take days, maybe weeks," said the redbeard. "Don't worry about them."

"I have to worry about them," she said without emotion. "They want to kill me every bit as much as they do you. I'm sure Andrew has told them that I've become your harlot. That alone would be enough, but I suspect there's a reward for me equal to that on you. Don't forget that we each represent a Barony."

"The day I forget it is the day you'd better find someone else to save your skin," he said. He walked over to a window and peered out into the blackness. "Can't see a damned thing."

"Then you think you might have been followed?" she

149

said quickly.

"It's possible," he admitted. "A running man in an empty street can make a lot of noise."

"Then perhaps we'd better leave now."

"There's no reason to. If they knew where I was, they'd have done something by now. Even if they heard me, they probably lost my trail a couple of miles back."

"I don't think so," said Alutha.

"What are you talking about?"

"I think we should get out of here right away."

"You're crazy."

"Please, Will."

"Rath, if that's what it'll take to make you keep quiet!" he muttered, opening the door.

They were less than a block away when they heard the steps echoing across the empty pavement. "Well, I'll be damned!" whispered the redbeard. He started off to the west, then saw a small group of men far ahead of him, and turned north. Once again he saw a party of armed men approaching.

He turned back in the direction of the rooms he had just quit, but the first group of men had passed them and was still advancing.

"We're in for it now," he whispered to Alutha, handing her his dagger and pulling out his warclub for himself.

It was obvious that they could see him now, though they didn't increase their pace. He took a momentary pride in the fact that his reputation made them reluctant to charge him, but it was only momentary, for he saw that he would soon be overwhelmed by sheer force of numbers.

They approached him from three directions, and he had no choice but to retreat in the one path open to him. They were narrowing the distance between them, and he yielded ground more rapidly.

"Will!" said Alutha urgently from somewhere behind him.

"Where in Rath have you been?" he said. "I thought you were beside me."

"I went ahead of you to see why they were herding us this way," she said rapidly. "They're trying to force us into a blind alley."

"A what?"

"A street that ends in a wall," she explained. "You can't let them do it."

"I'm open to suggestions," he said, still retreating.

"Try the group on your right," she said. "Charge them."

"Any particular reason why?" he asked, shooting them a quick glance.

"They just look easier than the rest," she said.

"But there are more of them," he protested.

"Try them anyway," she said, starting off in that direction.

There was no more time for words. He sensed the dead end coming up, and immediately turned to his right and raced toward the advancing Normals. There were seven men in the party. Five broke ranks and ran before his onslaught; the other two quickly fell victim to his warclub. Then they were in the open, racing down the street for the city's edge. The remaining Normals gave chase, but desperation gave Donahoe and Alutha added stamina if not additional speed, and within minutes they were safely out of Providence, zig-zagging crazily through the fields and woods beyond the ancient city.

"Nice guess," he wheezed when they had finally stopped running.

"Luck," she shrugged.

"That's twice you've been lucky for me. I think I'll keep you around as a charm whether I marry you or not."

"Don't do me any favors," she replied coldly.

Three weeks later they trudged into the remains of Hartford, which had been almost totally demolished in the war and was only sparsely populated. Communication

151

with other Normal cities and outposts was almost non-existent, and Donahoe and Alutha were immediately accepted without incident.

They were married the day they arrived, and Red Will Donahoe, for what very little it was worth, added another Barony to his collection.

CHAPTER TWENTY-THREE

—Rutting like animals! It's disgusting!

—If it bothers you so much, Jon, why don't you stop looking in at him?

—Somebody's got to keep tabs on him, Gareth. He's just about decided not to go back to the Hub until next spring, you know.

—Yes, I know. It's just as well. Craston is a very shrewd young man. I don't want him putting two and two together.

—Do you really think he could do you any harm?

—Nobody alive can do me any harm, Jon.

—But Craston could be a hindrance?

—Conceivably. That's why I'm going to make sure that the barbarian stays in Hartford for a while.

CHAPTER TWENTY-FOUR

They had been in Hartford less than two weeks when it happened.

They had shared the same roof and the same bed. Neither considered it anything but a political alliance, born of necessity and probably doomed to end in ignominy, but it served both their purposes for the present, and so they went through with it.

For her part, Alutha had yet to find the key to controlling him, though the occasional gift of her body tended to make him more tractable. For his part, Donahoe grudgingly conceded that Stramm was no longer the only Normal he felt any liking for.

Other changes were coming over him too. He had by no means given up his plan to return to the Hub and take power by whatever means were expedient, but he would not do so as a conquering invader. He had reconciled himself to the fact that he was a Normal, and quickly found that the cloak of Normalcy fitted his needs very well. Gareth Colle killed Normals; as one of the Normal Barons—ultimately the only one—the preservation of the race was his foremost duty, practically a sacred obligation. The next time he invaded the tunnels it wouldn't be with a mere four hundred men; he would march into Gareth's domain at the head of a column of tens of thousands. It was a pleasant thought. Being a Normal had its advantages.

Their first eleven days as man and wife, if not quite what most newlyweds dream about, were at least passably pleasant. Then came the twelfth day. It began as pleasantly as the others until Donahoe heard a commotion near the center of the ancient city. Curious, he rose from the bed, dressed quickly, and went out to see what was the matter.

". . . just appeared and then disappeared!" one of the townspeople was screaming hysterically. "I reached out for him and he was gone!"

"I think Jason's been out in the sun too long!" laughed another. "People don't just appear out of thin air and then vanish."

"I tell you I *saw* him!" shrieked Jason.

"What did he look like?" asked Donahoe, shouldering his way through the gathering throng of humanity.

"About your height, maybe an inch or two smaller," said Jason, calming down a bit. "A little slimmer. He just popped out of nothing and appeared right in front of me! Right out of the air! I know it sounds crazy, but . . ."

"What color was his hair?" asked the redbeard, trying to keep the apprehension out of his voice.

"Hair? Hair?" Jason closed his eyes, trying to conjure up a mental picture. "I remember now! He didn't have any hair. He was completely bald. I don't think he even had any eyebrows."

"Fantastic!" scoffed a bystander. "Jason, I think you've been drinking too much again."

"Or maybe all that girl-chasing has unhinged his mind!" laughed another.

They were still laughing when the redbeard finally made his way back to Alutha, who had followed him out and was standing at the back of the crowd.

"It's one of them, isn't it?" she asked tensely.

He nodded. "Raal."

"What does it mean?"

"It means that we're in for it," he said grimly.

"Isn't it possible that he was just checking up on your whereabouts?"

"Gareth doesn't need anyone to tell him where I am," said Donahoe. "No, Raal was scouting the territory, and

155

not for Gareth. There's going to be an attack."

"But I thought you said that Gareth never attacks Normal cities."

"He never has. This is the first time."

"But why?" she asked. "Why now?"

"There's only one reason I can think of," he said, suddenly exultant. "I'm getting close! I don't know what the secret is, but I'm getting close to it! He's scared now, scared of what I might do."

"Are you sure?" she said dubiously.

"Of course! Why else would he be coming after me? He's out to kill me, and he wouldn't be doing it if I wasn't close. Just think of it! He's afraid of me! After twenty lifetimes of playing God, Gareth Cole is afraid of me! *Of me!*"

"Then why doesn't he just kill you?" she asked, still skeptical. "Why mount an attack on the city?"

"I don't know. Maybe he can't kill me any longer. Maybe I'm so close to it that he doesn't dare try to kill me himself! Or maybe Stramm and Drake were right: maybe there really is a limit to what he can do with his creatures. Rath! Who cares? The important thing is that I'm too dangerous to keep alive, and we've got to figure out why before they get here."

But even as the words left his lips they arrived, flying, slithering, crawling, sliding, armed with spears, armed with arrows, a few of the more dangerous ones not armed at all.

The Normals were caught unprepared, but they fought back gamely, neither asking nor giving quarter. Donahoe shoved Alutha into a nearby doorway, then withdrew his warclub and jumped in among the army he once led, dealing bone-crushing blows to all who came within his reach. Jubal stood in his way, and then suddenly Jubal didn't possess three heads any longer. Jeremy, blinded by the sunlight, never saw the blow that killed him. Raal barely disappeared in time to avoid a sledge-

156

hammer blow that would have caved his skull in.

A moment later he was standing beside Jon. The golden youth sat cross-legged on the ground, his eyes closed, his senses dead to the world. Donahoe raised his warclub high in the air, but couldn't make himself bring it down upon his former lieutenant. Cursing himself for his softness, he flung himself back into the midst of the battle with renewed fury.

Most of the Normals were dead or dying. A few fought valiantly on, though it was obvious that the cause was lost. The redbeard felt a spear thud home into his calf, felt someone rip it out through layers of flesh and muscle, and then his balance gave out and he fell heavily to the ground. He could feel the blood spurting out, pouring down over his ankle. Then a heavy foot struck his temple and he could feel nothing more.

CHAPTER TWENTY-FIVE

"Stop babbling, man," said Craston, "and say it again slowly."

"Well," said Jason, "after this . . . this *thing* with no hair disappeared, it couldn't have been more than fifteen minutes before the whole goddamned bunch of them came at us. They were horrible, Baron Craston, just horrible!"

"I know, I know!" snapped Craston. "Get on with it."

"We were outnumbered. There can't have been much more than a thousand of us in the city, including the women." Jason's breathing became hard and heated at the memory of the slaughter, and he had to pause for a few moments while he regained his composure. His eyes were becoming used to Craston's dimly lit quarters, and he marveled that Baron Rysler could see well enough to be scribbling down notes at the table across the room. "Anyway, we fought them as best we could, and I guess we gave a pretty fair account of ourselves, but there were just too many of them."

"How many would you say you killed?" asked Rysler, looking up from his papers.

"Between three and four hundred," replied Jason. "But when it was over there were only nineteen Normal men left alive, and all but three of us were wounded."

"How about the women and children?" asked Rysler.

"Most of them are dead. A few—a very few—were unharmed."

"And you've come to ask for aid?"

"Yes, Baron. For medical aid. You see, we had only two doctors, and both of them were—"

"But why come to the Hub?" interrupted Craston.

"There are many other cities that are closer to you. What brought you here?"

"A few of the others have gone to the closer cities," said Jason, "but I thought you'd be especially willing to help, inasmuch as Baroness Drake is one of the survivors."

"Alutha is in Hartford?" exclaimed Craston, suddenly tense and alert. "You're sure it's Alutha Drake?"

"Yes," said Jason, "though she's married again."

"To a man with a red beard?"

"Yes. Will Donahoe, I believe his name is."

"Was he killed during the fighting?" demanded Craston.

"No, Baron," said Jason. "As I recall, he received a severe wound and is unable to walk, but he's alive."

"That will be all, Jason. Joshua will show you to a room, and we'll let you know our decision shortly."

No sooner had Jason departed then Craston was on his feet, pacing restlessly back and forth across the floor.

"Well, what do you make of it?" asked Rysler.

"I'm not sure yet," replied the blind Baron. "There are so many bits and pieces that it's hard to fit them all together."

"It seems rather simple to me," offered Rysler. "Cole tried to kill Donahoe and didn't quite succeed."

"Nonsense!" snapped Craston impatiently. "They could have killed him whenever they wanted. If he was crippled, any one of them could have administered the death blow."

"Then how do you explain the raid?"

"I can't—not yet, anyway. There are too many things that don't make sense. For example, why did Cole's army attack a Normal city in the first place? They've never done that before."

"Because Donahoe was there," said Rysler.

"That's only part of the answer," said Craston. "If Donahoe was all they wanted, they could easily have

159

killed or captured him. No, it's something more than that."

"Could it be that Cole has finally decided to take the offensive?" asked Rysler.

"Possibly," said Craston. "But why Hartford? It was an agrarian community with scarcely a thousand citizens. It's not hostile, it holds no strategic value, it doesn't even have any form of commerce with us. If I were Gareth Cole and I had decided to launch an active military campaign, I think Hartford would be just about the least desirable target on my list. No, Gerald, the only unique thing about Hartford that could possibly catch Cole's interest is that Donahoe was there. And yet, the battle is over, the mutants are victorious, and Donahoe is still alive and still in Hartford."

"It doesn't make any sense!" growled Rysler, throwing up his hands in exasperation. "There are too damn many facets of this thing that we just don't know!"

"Then let's examine what we do know," said Craston, sitting down once again. "We know the attack was made solely because Donahoe was there. We know that they were obviously under orders not to kill him. We know that Cole had no reservations about killing almost everyone else in the city."

"And that's all we know," said Rysler disgustedly.

"It's so damned frustrating!" shouted Craston suddenly. "There's something buried here, some secret I can't unearth. Gareth Cole has never done anything without a reason. What in hell's name was his motive? What did he hope to accomplish?" He groaned and smashed his hand down against his thigh. "It's like when I first woke up after Cole blinded me. I remember searching for my shoes. I knew they were there, easily within my reach, and yet I couldn't find them. The harder I looked the more elusive they seemed to become. I must have groped around in this infernal blackness for an hour before my hands finally made

160

contact with them. And even then I couldn't see to buckle them." He paused. "Damn it! There's a reason for all this hidden here somewhere, but I can't find it!"

"Maybe it would be best to wait for his next move," suggested Rysler.

"How can we prepare for his next move if we can't understand his current one?" snapped Craston. "We've got to figure it out, and it's get to be done fast, before we're attacked from both sides."

"I don't follow you," said Rysler.

"It's as plain as the nose on your face. Along with everything else, Cole doubtless intends to have Donahoe come back here and take over the other Baronies."

"I don't know how you can deduce that from the simple fact that he let Donahoe live."

"I can't," agreed Craston. "But I *can* deduce it from the singular fact that he let Alutha live."

CHAPTER TWENTY-SIX

It was three months before he was able to walk without help, and two more before his limp vanished completely. Outwardly he chafed with impatience at being confined to his bed and later his room, but actually he found himself almost enjoying the total relief from the pressures of conflict. So at peace was he that when Alutha fearfully informed him that she was pregnant, he found himself quite able to contain his rage at having an increasingly helpless woman to care for, and actually began looking forward eagerly to the birth of his child. His drinking and cursing tapered off somewhat, and with Alutha's prodding he took the time to read a couple of books before the mental strain caused him to throw the remaining stack of literature away in disgust.

Almost every evening they sat by a fire and talked, and with precious few exceptions the subject matter of their conversations never varied. This particular evening was no different.

"Go over it again, Will," said Alutha, drawing meaningless geometric figures on a pad of paper.

"When we were about half a mile beyond the Holland Tunnel," he repeated, almost by rote, "Raal appeared in front of us."

"Just as he did before they attacked the village?"

"I've only told you that a thousand times!" he growled. "He appeared, took a look, and then vanished. Nothing else happened for a minute or two, and then one of Gareth's monsters jumped me. After that, the whole damned Tunnel was filled with them in a matter of minutes."

"And you're sure Raal wasn't appraising your strength and reporting back to Gareth?"

"Of course not! Gareth didn't have to send anybody to tell him how many men I had and what we were doing. He sent Raal just to scare the Normals, and except for Stramm, I think it worked pretty well."

"Then we get back to the crux of the matter," she sighed, tired of going over it point by point, night after night, but certain that the answer lay hidden in there somewhere and determined to find it. "Why were you able to kill the monsters?"

"We were stronger."

"That's not a good enough answer, Will," said Alutha wearily. "Ultimately you were defeated."

"I don't know!" he snapped. "Maybe he was just toying with us!"

"That won't do. I know it's the logical answer, but it just won't do. There's got to be some better reason."

"Don't you think I know that?" demanded the redbeard. "I've been trying to figure it out for half a year!"

"I'm sorry, Will," she said. "I didn't mean to upset you. It's just that . . ." Her voice trailed off into silence. She closed her eyes and leaned her head down onto the table in front of her.

"I'm sorry too," he said gently. "But we haven't been able to figure it out for the past hundred nights, and I don't think the next hundred are going to be any easier." He paused. "Zameth! It's driving me crazy! I can hurt him—I know I can! I've done it twice already, and I still don't know why or how! Maybe I'm right. Maybe he *is* just leading me on for the hell of it!"

"When you were a child, growing up in the subways," she said, sitting erect again, "did anyone else ever challenge him as you've done? Was he ever known to feel pain?"

"Oh, he feels pain, all right," said Donahoe. "I used to laugh at it. Here he was, some kind of god with

163

all those damned powers of his, and it took every ounce of strength he had just to keep that puny body of his alive. He was always coughing from a cold, or half dead with some virus or other. But as for any *person* inflicting pain, forget it. They're all on his side."

"Wasn't anyone ever dissatisfied?"

"Not that I know of. If they were, I'm sure he took care of them. Every once in a while one of them would vanish. I never knew what had happened, but all those damned mindreaders never got too upset over it, so I imagine Gareth told them whatever he wanted them to know—the truth, probably—and nothing came of it."

"Then it's possible that he *was* challenged on occasion," she persisted.

"It's possible, yes, but not likely. And he was never hurt."

"Did you ever hurt any of his creatures while you were living there?"

"No. The first time was during the last invasion, when I threw my warclub at one of the firebirds and it didn't vanish in time. And then there was the battle in the tunnels."

"Had you ever tried to hurt one of the firebirds before?"

"Hundreds of times. When I was a kid I made a slingshot and used to take pot shots at them."

"But you never hurt them?"

"No," admitted Donahoe, "I never did. Either they'd vanish, or else the rocks would bounce off them."

"Think hard, Will," she urged him. "What did you do differently the time you hit the firebird? What did you do that you hadn't done any other time?"

"Nothing! Not a damned thing!" He slammed a fist down on the table. "'I didn't do a damned thing differently. I had just come out of the water and directed Gareth's freaks to start shooting their arrows into the

Normans—the Normals—and after we won I saw the firebird and threw my club at it."

"What were you doing in the water?"

"You know damned well what I was doing there! I had set fire to the boats and I had to get away."

"Maybe it was the water," she said, knowing that it wasn't but unable to restrain herself from grasping at straws.

"I picked up the warclub from a corpse after I got out of the water," he said. "And besides, there wasn't any water during the fight in the tunnels."

"What *was* in the tunnels that was also present when you hurt the firebird?"

"Nothing!" he bellowed, rising and stalking back and forth across the room. "Once I was with the Normals, once I was with the freaks. Once I used a dead man's warclub, once I used my hands. Once I was outside, once I was inside. Once the firebird was trying to help me, once the monsters were trying to kill me. Once Gareth was miles away, once he was within a couple of hundred yards. The only damned thing they had in common was that both times Gareth got me alone and told me he could take anything I could dish out. Who knows?" he concluded in a disgusted mutter. "Maybe he can."

"Are you sure that was the *only* thing he told you?" she insisted. "Did he just say that and walk away?"

"No, of course not," replied Donahoe irritably. "But that was the gist of it."

"Why did he even bother talking to you?" she mused, half to herself. "Why not kill you and have done with it?"

"I don't know. He says I need him."

"That *you* need *him?*" she repeated quickly. "I thought you told me last week that he said you needed each other."

"He did," said the redbeard. "What in Rath is the difference? Gareth never needed anybody. Maybe he just said it to make me feel important, or to keep me out of his hair."

"No, he meant it all right. Otherwise you'd have been dead years ago."

"Why does he keep a Normal alive?" he asked. "Even if I did grow up in the tunnels, I'm still a Normal, as much as you and Craston and the rest. I have no powers of any kind—you know it, I know it, and he knows it. What can he want from me?"

"Maybe if we can figure that out we'll know how to defeat him," said Alutha.

"We'll do it anyway!" snapped the redbeard, his eyes glowing like coals. "So help me, I'll kill him with my bare hands!" The hatred came pouring back into him now, as he paced faster and faster. A steady stream of obscenities flowed from his lips, and finally he stalked out into the night.

Alutha knew that another session was over. Sooner or later every discussion of Gareth Cole ended like this. In many ways he had mellowed during his recuperation, but any prolonged talk of Cole and his defeat ultimately brought back every last vestige of barbarism that Donahoe had tried to cast aside.

He didn't return until noon of the next day, at which time he perfunctorily announced that they were leaving Hartford.

"We're too damned far away," he said. "It's time to move out and get a little closer."

"Closer? Closer to what?"

"To Gareth. We're not going to be able to do him any harm sitting here in this ghost town talking about killing him. We'll have to get to where we can do something about it."

"But why now?" she asked. "Why today?"

"I think my leg's finally strong enough," he answered. "And if we wait much longer, you'll be too far along in your pregnancy to travel."

"Where are you planning to move to?"

"Waterbury, or maybe New Haven," said Donahoe. "A little closer to Gareth, and a little farther from Craston."

"Why worry about Andrew?" she asked.

"I'm not worried, but it makes sense that if Hartford didn't know about us, neither will Waterbury or New Haven."

She could see that protesting would do no good, and so she resignedly packed her few belongings into a cloth bag, and within an hour the pair of them were walking down a long-abandoned highway toward the southeast. Their progress was slow, for his leg was not quite as strong as he had believed, but by the end of the second day they were more than halfway to their destination. Then, as twilight approached, they armed themselves with crudely made bows and arrows and went out hunting for dinner. Donahoe had wanted a rabbit, but missed the first two he flushed. Disgusted with his lack of accuracy, he picked up a small rock and hurled it at a distant tree. There was a sudden flapping of wings and a large hawk flew out. The red-beard immediately fitted an arrow to his bow, took aim and let fly. The shaft plunged deep into the bird's breast, and with a final agonized squawk it fell to the ground, stone dead.

Alutha had been standing motionless, watching the bird's death dive with an expression of growing excitement. Suddenly she turned to Donahoe.

"Will, you can go on to New Haven if you want, or we can go back to Hartford. I'd prefer New Haven, I suppose, since there will be a doctor there, but it really doesn't matter any more."

"What in blazes are you talking about?" he growled, retrieving the hawk and returning to her.

"You'll be a hunted man now, no matter where you go. He'll stop at nothing to kill you, and me too, for that matter."

"Who will?"

"Cole. You see, *I know what Gareth Cole's weakness is!*"

CHAPTER TWENTY-SEVEN

—She knows, Gareth.

—That's not surprising, Jon. Sooner or later she had to figure it out.

—She's about to tell him. Don't you want to stop her?

—Why bother? They're in no position to do anything about it.

—But they can get help.

—Craston? He'll kill them on sight.

—All right. But I still don't like it, Gareth.

—Don't worry about it, Jon. Let him toy with this problem and he'll forget all about the bigger one.

CHAPTER TWENTY-EIGHT

"It's all so simple!" she exclaimed. "It's been staring us right in the face and we never saw it!"

"Come on, woman!" said the redbeard. "What's it all about?"

"It's so simple!" she repeated. "We've been trying to open the jar from the wrong end!"

"Will you stop talking in circles and tell me what you've figured out!" he growled, angrily throwing the hawk to the ground.

"Listen, Will," said Alutha. "We know that you were able to hurt him—or at least his creatures—twice. The problem was that we couldn't figure out what you had done both of those times that you hadn't done on other occasions that enabled you to harm him."

"You've figured out what I did!" he exclaimed.

"*You* didn't do anything," she said. "That's what I meant when I said we've been attacking this the wrong way."

"What do you mean?"

"You didn't do anything—*but Gareth did!*"

"Gareth?" he repeated, puzzled. "What did *he* do?"

"Think about it," she urged him. "When you first hurled a rock at the bird on the day of the last invasion attempt, you said that it vanished. Yet an hour later you threw a club at it and almost killed it. Why? What was different the second time than the first?"

"I don't know. What was?"

"Will, how did you set fire to those boats?" she asked him. "If you had to fight your way there, you couldn't possibly have had time to light the fire yourself."

"I didn't," he said.

"Then how did you manage to get the fire going?"

"One of the firebirds set it for me."

"And that's the answer!" she said triumphantly.

"I don't understand."

"When you threw the first rock at the firebird, that bird was the only thing Gareth was controlling."

"There was only a single bird the second time, when I hit it," protested the redbeard.

"There was only one bird," she agreed, "but there were eight different fires!" He stared mutely at her, "Don't you see? When all Gareth had to control was a single firebird, it was invincible—but when he had to manage the bird *plus* the fires, he couldn't protect or handle everything at once. And since the fires were more important—"

"—he left the bird unguarded! That's it!" yelled the redbeard. "That's got to be it! It explains everything. That's why we could kill dozens of monsters in the caves, but when he fought back with a single creature, it demolished us!"

"That's right, Will," she said, calming down somewhat. "And that's how Gareth Cole can be defeated—by attacking him from so many directions that he can't possibly control everything at once!"

"I don't know," said the redbeard. "All he'd have to do would be create a single creature instead of a lot of them, and . . ."

"It wouldn't work, Will. Don't forget: your army was small in numbers, and was confined to a single area. Attack him aith twenty thousand men, completely encircle and permeate the subways, and no single monster can possibly protect him. He'll need hundreds of them, and the more he creates, the less powerful they'll be. Look at it this way—can any Normal swordsman, even a brilliant one, defeat you in battle?"

"No!"

"But what if two mediocre swordsmen approached you from different sides? Could you fend them off?"

"Not unless I rushed one of them," he admitted.

"And if you were completely surrounded, would even rushing them do you any good?"

"No. My only hope would be to break through their lines."

"And Gareth won't even be able to do that! The moment his monsters break through our lines, he'll be unprotected! We'll just keep him so busy that he can't defend himself on all sides."

"I think you've got it!"

"I know I do."

"How did you figure it out?" he asked her.

"I don't know. I just saw the hawk plummeting to the ground the way you said the firebird did, and suddenly everything was clear."

"I don't imagine everything is clear insofar as rounding up a Normal army is concerned."

"We'll start by sending a note to Andrew and Gerald," she said.

"Fat lot of good that'll do us," he muttered.

"When we've told them that we've discovered the way to destroy Gareth Cole, I think they'll at least be willing to listen."

"And the second we've told them how to do it, they'll kill us," said Donahoe.

"Not if you relinquish your claim to the Baronies."

"They're mine!" he roared. "I won them and I'll keep them!"

"What's more important to you—being a hunted would-be Baron, or defeating Gareth Cole?"

He glowered at her for a moment, then shrugged. "All right. Tell Craston he can have the damned castles."

"Good," she said. "Now we'd better get to a city and send the message off while there's still time."

"One thing," said the redbeard, picking up the hawk again.

"Yes."

"They've got to agree that I'll be the one to kill Gareth. Otherwise, they can roast in Rath before we'll meet with them!"

CHAPTER TWENTY-NINE

They didn't send the note immediately. In fact, they were lucky to send it, or to reach New Haven, at all. The redbeard's injured leg, seemingly as good as new, was not up to the demands he was making upon it. The wound reopened, infection set it, the leg bloated up to double its size, and it was all Alutha could do to keep him alive. For almost two weeks he was delirious with fever, and it was another twelve weeks before they could continue their trek.

The last few weeks were especially hard on them, for Alutha's pregnancy had progressed to the point where she was unable to go far enough afield to hunt effectively, and so they lived solely on fruits and such vegetables as they could find. Soon even these became sparse, and after a single day of eating tree bark, Donahoe declared that he was ready to go on towards their goal. Between her pregnancy and his leg, the remainder of the trip took the better part of two weeks, but at last they arrived in New Haven, where the note was immediately sent off to Craston and Rysler.

Once again the redbeard sensed a hint of the contentment that might be his after Cole was disposed of. As the companion of a Baroness, he found all of his needs provided for. His days were long and pleasant, his nights peaceful and occasionally passionate. He read another book, this time with no urging from Alutha, and took a few days off to build a crib for his son. (It never occurred to him that Alutha might possibly present him with a daughter. It would be a son, tall and rawboned and alert, and perhaps, he thought wistfully, just a shade more civilized than himself.)

He drew diagrams of the entire subway system, changing them from time to time as he remembered more entrances and exits, more connecting tunnels. He planned how each segment of his army would attack, how he would coordinate the entire battle so that Cole couldn't possibly operate with any effectiveness, and always, always, he planned what he would do when, after a lifetime filled with futile attempts, he finally got his hands on the blond mutant.

Yes, they were pleasant days, days in which he had nothing to do but plan his future, wait for Craston's reply, and await the birth of his child.

CHAPTER THIRTY

"Well, Gerald, what do you make of it?" asked Craston, after Rysler had read him the note.

"It's Alutha's handwriting, there's no doubt of that," came the reply.

"Of course it is," said Craston impatiently. "And it stands to reason that they'd be in New Haven. There's almost no one left alive in Hartford, and they could safely assume that New Haven would be unaware of the fact that we are looking for them."

"Then I don't quite understand your question," said Rysler.

"I mean, what's your opinion? Do you think it's a trap?"

"It could be," said Rysler, "but I doubt it. After all, they've told us where to find them. If we distrusted the note, we could take our armies with us for protection."

"My feelings precisely. Of course, there's always the possibility that it's a ruse to get us to do just that while Donahoe marches on the Hub and takes over all five Baronies, but I rather doubt that he's been able to gather a large enough force of men to do so, and surely he knows we wouldn't leave our properties completely unprotected and defenseless. No, I think we can safely assume that it's not a trap, which leads us to our next question: does he really know how to defeat Cole?"

"I'm inclined to think he doesn't," said Rysler, sipping a goblet of wine. "After all, he thought he could beat him when he went there with Elston and Aldan, and look what happened."

"Possibly he's learned what he did wrong," said Craston softly.

"I disagree," said Rysler. "If he really knows how to defeat Gareth Cole, why hasn't he done so already?"

"Obviously he needs help, and he seems to think that we'll be willing to come to his aid."

"What makes him think so?"

"That little offer he made," replied Craston. "He must be pretty sure he's right if he's willing to state in writing that he'll give up his claim to the Baronies if we'll help him."

"I think that's meaningless," said Rysler firmly. "If we really do defeat Cole, Donahoe will probably lead his former army against us and try to conquer the Hub."

Craston uttered a harsh laugh. "Do you really think we can get close to Cole before every last mutant is dead? No, Gerald, if we kill Cole, there won't be any mutant army left for Donahoe to lead."

"Then what's his game?" demanded Rysler. "What's he up to?"

"Did it ever occur to you that he just might be telling the truth?" responded Craston. "Can't you conceive of the possibility that he has really discovered the way to destroy Gareth Cole, and is willing to trade the promise of a Barony to accomplish his goal?"

"Then you think the letter is legitimate?"

"As a matter of fact, I do. As Elston once said, subtlety is not one of Donahoe's virtues—and I never knew it to be one of Alutha's either."

"Are you trying to tell me that Donahoe has actually figured out a way to beat Cole?" demanded Rysler unbelievingly.

"I am. And Donahoe is the only man in the world who could possibly have done so."

"Why do you say that?"

"He wrote us a letter in which he states that he has discovered Cole's weakness. Obviously he knows we will do everything we can to figure out just what that weakness is, and just as obviously he is totally confident that it can't be done. Therefore, whatever Cole's flaw is, it is of such a nature that only Donahoe, by virtue of his experience alone, could have hit upon it."

"Then you don't even propose to try?"

"Why bother?" answered Craston. "If you were to hand me a book, I would know what it was, but my blindness would prevent me from reading it. Donahoe has us in much the same situation. We know he has the solution, but by not having been with him every minute of his life, our blindness in that area prevents us from seeing how the solution may be arrived at. Only Donahoe knows what it is. Only Donahoe *can* know, and so he's quite willing to let us play around with an insufficient amount of data."

"So you think we should go to New Haven?"

"I imagine so," said Craston. "That letter is too damned confident. He's got the answer, all right, and he's sure of it. He knows what we can do to him now that we know where he is, and he's willing to risk it. I think we'd better face up to the fact that our mutant friend has got us over a barrel."

"I hear he's calling himself a Normal now," said Rysler, "and that he's legally married to Alutha. That's what scares me, Andrew. Even if he keeps his word, what's to stop him from siring a bunch of hell-born brats and letting one of them claim the vacant Baronies for him?"

"We'll worry about his hell-born brats, as you so delicate phrase it, when we come to them," said Craston. "The first step is to find out how to defeat Cole." Rysler said nothing, and Craston, after waiting a reasonable length of time for a reply, frowned. "You still don't like the thought of meeting with him, do you, Gerald?"

"Frankly, I don't," said Rysler. "I agree with you that

he's not trying to lead us into a trap, and I'm even willing to concede that he believes he's come up with the right answer. But if he really knows the way to destroy Cole, then—"

"I told you," interrupted Craston. "He can't do it alone. That's why he needs our help."

"You didn't let me finish," said Rysler patiently. "I was about to say that if he really knows the way to destroy Cole, then Cole would never have let him live to write that letter. If he had finally begun to present a danger to Cole's existence, then it would have been time for Cole to put an end to him."

"I never thought of that," admitted Craston. "Of course, Cole wouldn't let him live, unless . . . *unless!*" He jumped up, his entire body rigid, his sightless eyes staring excitedly into space.

"Andrew!" exclaimed Rysler, rushing over to him. "Andrew, are you all right?"

"I've got it?" shouted Craston. "It all fits together now!"

"You've figured it out?" said Rysler excitedly. "You know what Donahoe knows?"

"No," said Craston, lowering his voice to a whisper. "*I know what Donahoe hasn't even begun to guess!*"

"What are you getting at, Andrew?"

"I understand everything. Do you know why Gareth Cole attacked Hartford?"

"To kill Donahoe."

"You're wrong, Gerald," whispered Craston. "He did it to protect him."

"Protect him?" repeated Rysler. "From whom?"

"*From you and me, Gerald.* We were going to kill him, remember? Oh, God, now I understand!"

"Understand what?" demanded Rysler, perplexity making his temper rise.

"Don't ask me, Gerald. I can't mention it. I can't

ever think of it. I don't know how, but I've got to hide what I know from Gareth Cole until we can get to Donahoe."

"What do you intend to do with him—kill him?" asked Rysler, suddenly very frightened by Craston's intensity.

"Kill him?" Craston laughed hysterically. "Kill him? *He and I are the only two people on earth who can save what's left of the human race!*"

CHAPTER THIRTY-ONE

The tavern was crowded, for Red Will Donahoe was buying the drinks. Perhaps a few men in the barroom thought that he was being a bit premature and that his proper place was just outside the door to Alutha's room. They may have felt that no husband should be so carefree and exuberant while his wife was in labor, but if so, their feelings didn't prevent them from accepting the ale and liquor that flowed so freely.

It was cold out, bitter cold, and the weather served to make the rowdy group within the tavern even more closely-knit, as if this were the final outpost of the world and only here could the forces of mankind combat the forces of an embittered Nature.

Donahoe himself was feeling no pain. He had already downed half a dozen mugs of ale, and felt quite competent to pour another dozen down his throat before seeing how Alutha was coming along. Women had always had babies without much fuss and bother, and he was sure Alutha was equal to the best of them.

The next hour and the next gallon both passed quickly, and then a lone woman, middle-aged, graying, obviously tired, entered the tavern. Donahoe saw her and shouldered his way across the room toward her.

"Well?" he said in a loud voice, as the rest of the revellers fell silent.

"You're a father," she smiled.

"Damn it, woman!" he roared. "I know I'm a father! What did she have?"

"A son."

"A son!" he cried triumphantly. "I knew it! A son! Set 'em up again—I'm still buying."

There was a rush to the bar.

"What does he look like?" asked Donahoe eagerly.

"He's perfectly strong and healthy," replied the midwife. "And it looks like he's going to have a head of hair as red as yours."

"Oh-oh!" laughed one of the drinkers. "That's bad, Will. You'd better watch that kid's temper!"

"Wouldn't want a kid without any spunk!" shot back the redbeard. "That kid's going to have a little fire in him if I've anything to say about it."

"What are you going to name him?" asked another.

"I don't know," said Donahoe. "I haven't decided."

"Just make sure you don't have to name him after a grandparent," said a third one. "Every time I curse my wife's mother my daughter starts bawling!"

"No need to worry about that," said Donahoe softly. "I never knew who my parents were."

"Oh," said the man, flustered. "I'm sorry."

"No need to be. I don't think I would have liked them." He walked back to the bar and slammed his first down on it. "Well," he roared, "what are we waiting for? Let's drink up!"

The silence departed as quickly as it had arrived, to be replaced once more by laughter and the sounds of comradery. Donahoe drank another glass of ale, then turned to the midwife, who was still standing by the entrance.

"Come over and have a drink!" he yelled to her. "You earned it!"

"Don't you want to see your son?" she asked.

"Can I?" he asked, trying to hide his eagerness. "I didn't know I was allowed to so soon."

"Of course you can," she replied. "You're the father, aren't you?"

"That's why he wants to see the kid—to make sure!" guffawed one of the drinkers.

Donahoe felt his anger mounting, then realized that it was meant only as a joke, and joined in the laughter. "Can I go over now?" he asked.

"Certainly," said the midwife. "That's why I came here."

"Thanks," he said. "Listen, would it be all right if you kind of stayed around here for a while? Just a few minutes. I'd like to . . . well . . ."

"I understand," she smiled. "I'll be back in about half an hour."

He gave her a kiss on the cheek, carried her over to the bar and sat her down on it, and walked out into the freezing night.

As he approached their house he became more and more excited. A son—and with red hair, too! He had never guessed how much a son would mean to him. Even during Alutha's long hours of labor he had been able to maintain his calm. It was only now, now that it was actually over and he could hold his son in his own arms, that he realized how very happy he was, how much he had looked forward to this moment. It was almost as if his life was now complete . . .

And then, with a feeling of sickening revulsion, he knew.

There was no time to question it, barely time to act at all. He ran the rest of the way and burst into the room. Alutha, who should have been in bed, was on her feet, staring at him like some wild animal fighting for its life.

"You're going to kill him, aren't you?" she shrieked, racing across the room and clawing at his face with her nails.

"Get away!" he snapped, thrusting her against a wall with a sweep of his hand. He pulled out his warclub, strode quickly to the tiny crib that held an even tinier particle of humanity, and brought the club down on

183

the infant's head. There was one piteous wail, and then the flicker of life so recently brought into the world was stilled forever.

He turned back to Alutha. She sat on the floor, propped up against a wall, staring dully at the blood that was beginning to drip from the crib.

"Why?" she asked in a lifeless monotone. "Why did you do it?"

"I had to." He began trembling so violently that he had to wait until it subsided before he was able to speak again. "I had to, when I realized why Gareth Cole was keeping me alive."

"Why?" she repeated dully, the tears beginning to fill her face, then overflowing and streaming down her ashen face.

"Don't you see?" he asked in a tortured, strangled voice. "Why did Gareth let me live? He's stronger than I am, he's smarter than I am, he has powers no man has ever dreamed of. What is the only thing I have that he could possibly need?"

"I don't know," she said, staring at the dripping blood as if hypnotized.

"*My genes!*" he said. "*Gareth Cole needed my genes to produce this child for him!* I can call myself a Normal until Rath freezes over, but I'm not! My parents were mutants, and I carry their blood in my veins. I may not have any powers, but I'm as much of a mutant as Gareth Cole!*"

"Liar!" she rasped, rising to her feet and flailing away weakly at his chest. "Liar! Liar!"

"It's true!" he said, pinning her arms to her sides. "It's got to be true! That's the only reason he could possibly have for letting me survive!"

"Liar!" she screamed. "How many Normal women have you raped? How many hundreds of bastards have you fathered? Why did you have to kill this one?"

"*Because you're a mutant too!*"

"No!"

He shook her violently, trying to make her understand. "You are! You're as out of place in a Normal society as I was in the tunnels!"

"It's not true!" she sobbed. "I have no powers! You killed him for nothing!"

"You *do* have a power," he said, lowering his voice.

"Liar!"

"How did you know I was going to kill him?" he demanded.

"I could tell by your face," she wept.

"Like Rath you could! You were on your feet, ready to protect him, even before I entered the room!"

"And you did it anyway!" she screamed. "You murdered my lover and you murdered my father and now you've murdered my baby!"

"Listen to me!" he yelled at her. "That day we escaped from the Hub—how did you know where Craston's men would be? Or the time you knew four of Rysler's warriors were waiting on the trail ahead of us. What made you think they were there? Or our escape from Providence, or even the way you discovered Gareth's weakness?"

"I don't know!" she sobbed, collapsing weakly onto the bed. "I don't know!"

"*I* know. Call it second sight, hunching, or anything else you want—but it's a power no Normal has. You're a mutant. You're as much of a freak as Gareth and me!"

"But why me?" she mumbled. "Why my baby? He was so tiny, so pink and helpless. What power could he have had? What harm could he have done?"

"I don't know," admitted the redbeard. "I don't think we'll ever know. It's enough that Gareth needed him, needed him badly enough to keep me alive all these years."

Suddenly she sat up, her eyes flaming with hatred,

185

her body tense. "You're wrong!"

"No I'm not," he said gently. "Think about it and you'll know I'm not."

"If all he wanted was the baby, *then why are you still alive?* Why didn't he kill you the day it was conceived?"

"I don't know. He probably let me live to protect you until it was born, or to conceive another if you miscarried. Or maybe he was afraid you'd guess his purpose. That's probably why he attacked Hartford—to make sure we couldn't return to the Hub until the baby was conceived and born. Maybe he knew Craston would figure it out the second he discovered you were pregnant. It was very carefully planned. He plotted my whole life so that I would wind up killing Drake and marrying you. Maybe that's why—"

"You're guessing!" she screamed. "You've murdered my baby, and now you're grabbing at straws to prove you're right! Murderer!"

She began hitting and scratching him again, and then it happened.

He didn't mean to hurt her. It was only a reflex action, instinctively committed as he tried to ward off her blows. He meant only to push her back out of reach, but an instant later her body slammed into the wall, and her head struck the edge of the heavy wooden bed frame as she fell.

He knew she was dead before he knelt down to examine her. Unlike the baby, there was no blood; but like the baby, there was no life either.

The midwife would be coming back shortly, he knew, if the commotion hadn't already brought a number of neighbors on the run. And once again he would be an outcast, hunted by mutant and Normal alike, fleeing from forest to marsh, avoiding all human and superhuman life. Sooner or later one side or the other would catch him, of that he was sure; but the instinct to life was strong in him, and he prepared to get away and stay alive as best he could.

He looked down at Alutha one last time. Then, slowly, tenderly, he leaned down and kissed her, something he had never done before despite all the many times he had used her body.

Then, with a guttural sound midway between a grunt and a sob, he raced out into the frozen night.

CHAPTER THIRTY-TWO

"What's the problem?" demanded Craston, drawing his cloak more tightly around his shoulders. "Why are we slowing down?"

"Something's wrong," said Rysler. "There's a big crowd gathered around his house."

"Find out what happened!" said Craston excitedly.

Rysler called one of the townspeople over. "What's going on?" he asked.

"Murder!" yelled the man. "Donahoe must have gone berserk! We're just about to go out after him!"

"Who's dead?" asked Craston.

"His wife and his baby. God, what a sight! The poor thing couldn't have been half an hour old!"

"You're sure they're dead?" insisted the blind Baron.

"*Sure?*" repeated the man, half hysterically. "There's nothing left of that baby above the neck! God, are we going to make him suffer for this!" The man ran off after his companions.

"Then we're too late," said Rysler dejectedly.

"On the contrary," said Craston. "Donahoe solved the puzzle without my help."

"Solved the puzzle?" repeated Rysler with a look of horror. "You mean you *wanted* him to kill them?"

"It was the only way to save the race," said Craston. "But why?"

"Because Gareth Cole wanted that child," said Craston slowly. "He wanted him enough to destroy almost the entire population of Hartford, and he needed him enough so that he couldn't conquer the Normals without him."

"How do you know?" demanded Rysler, still shocked by the brutality of Donahoe's act and the pleasure with which his blind compatriot accepted it.

"What else could it be?" said Craston. "We knew from the start that Donahoe had no mutated powers, but the safety we felt from that knowledge dulled our reasoning processes. We forgot that he was a mutant nonetheless. And why should Cole keep a powerless mutant around—especially one who consistently tried to depose him? Only for his offspring."

"But I know of seven different Normal women who bore his children. What makes either of you think that Alutha was the one woman who would produce what Cole wanted?"

"It was easier for Donahoe to figure that out," explained Craston. "After all, he lived with her. Possibly she was a mutant produced by Normal parents, just as Cole was; possibly he saw something else in her that convinced him that she was the woman Cole had selected for him. Whatever the reason, he saw it and recognized it for what it was."

"But you don't even know what Donahoe saw in her," protested Rysler. "How were you able to come up with the same conclusion?"

"Donahoe's note provided the final clue," said the blind Baron.

"In what way?"

"Remember what I told you after the slaughter at Hartford—that Cole hadn't killed Alutha because he meant for her and Donahoe to come back to the Hub and claim the Baronies? Well, when Donahoe offered to give up his right to the Baronies in his note to us, I realized that I had been wrong—that Cole had no intention of having Donahoe push us out of power. And if that was so, then there could have been only one reason why he let Alutha survive that attack. He might have wanted to keep Donahoe alive for any of a hundred different reasons, but there was only one reason to let Alutha live: to produce a child."

"I see," said Rysler, letting loose a low whistle. "Now that it's done, is there any way we can find out what they knew about Cole?"

"Not a chance," said Craston. "Donahoe is the only man who knows how to defeat Cole, and Cole no longer has any reason to keep Donahoe alive. He's got to kill him now, before Donahoe does any more damage. In fact, I'd be willing to bet that Donahoe is already dead."

"Then we're back where we started."

"Not exactly, Gerald," said the blind Baron. "We may not know Donahoe's method of defeating him, but we know something even more important: we know that Gareth Cole was unwilling to act until the child was born. What we have to do is figure out why he needed that child before he discovers a way to replace him. The battle lines have been drawn," he concluded with a grim smile. "It should prove most interesting."

CHAPTER THIRTY-THREE

He was running.

He did not know how long he had been running or where he was, but he knew they would be after him and so he forced himself to continue, unmindful of the pain in his leg and the merciless agony in his ribs that came with every breath he took. His face was streaked with tears; some had come from grief, others from the icy wind. He paid no attention to either.

His leg finally gave out near dawn and, panting painfully, he threw himself to the ground, gulping the cold air into his tortured lungs. Now even the throbbing in his leg was gone, replaced by an all-encompassing numbness.

He forced himself to stand after a few minutes, knowing that if he lay down much longer he would soon fall asleep, and if he did so he would never awaken. He listened carefully for sounds of pursuit, though he wasn't worried about the men he knew would be chasing him, hunting him down like a mad animal. It was Gareth he feared, and it was Gareth he could not understand.

Why hadn't Gareth come after him yet? He could be of no further use to him now that Alutha was dead. Moreover, he was a definite menace with the knowledge he possessed.

Ultimately he could not force the thought from his mind any longer. Could he possibly have been wrong? Was Alutha right when she screamed that he was grasping at straws, trying to invent a justification after committing an unbelievably horrible blunder? Was his son everything he had hoped for, rather than some monster even Gareth Cole would have to bow down to?

No, it couldn't be! He shook himself violently, as if physically trying to hurl the nagging fear away. And yet, if he had been right, if the child had to die, then where was Gareth? Why did he still live? Was he truly the savior of the race, or was he a bloodier butcher than ever Alutha could have imagined?

He cursed the thought, battled with it, but could not force it from his mind. Finally he yielded to it, allowed it to remain with him, and turned his face into the east wind. The sun was beginning to rise, and he knew he would have to start running once more.

Then he stared toward the rising sun again and blinked his eyes furiously. Something was up there, floating effortlessly across the sky. As it drew near a sense of elation overwhelmed him.

"I was right!" he roared.

The firebird hovered above him for an instant, then swooped gracefully down for the kill.

"I was right!" he yelled again. "Damn you, Gareth, I was right!"

Long after the firebird had completed its mission, the redbeard's triumphant cry still echoed through the icy air.